Anonymous

Lyntonville or the Irish boy in Canada

Anonymous

Lyntonville or the Irish boy in Canada

ISBN/EAN: 9783744738262

Printed in Europe, USA, Canada, Australia, Japan

Cover: Foto ©Andreas Hilbeck / pixelio.de

More available books at **www.hansebooks.com**

HARDY'S KNIFE FOUND.

LYNTONVILLE;

OR,

The Irish Boy in Canada.

London:

THE RELIGIOUS TRACT SOCIETY,

56, PATERNOSTER ROW;

65, ST. PAUL'S CHURCHYARD; & 164, PICCADILLY.

CONTENTS.

CONTENTS.

CHAPTER VII.

CHAPTER VIII.

CHAPTER IX.

CHAPTER X.

CHAPTER XI.

CHAPTER XII.

LYNTONVILLE.

CHAPTER I.

LYNTONVILLE.

" Thou, who hast given me eyes to see,
    And love this sight so fair,
  Give me a heart to find out Thee,
    And read Thee everywhere."

LYNTONVILLE was the name of a large old-fashioned log-house which stood embosomed amongst the tall trees of a Canadian forest, where sombre balsams and hacmatacs* mingled their dark foliage with the silvery birch and maple. Delicate buds and blossoms peeped out from beneath their rugged stems, or uprooted trunks; and feathery ferns lurked in hidden nooks and corners in the woods all around it. There, too, the squirrels frisked about, and the little chip-muncks† chirped merrily as they played at hide-and-seek amongst the branches.

---

* The Indian name of the American larch, sometimes called the cypress.
  † A small striped squirrel.

" The house itself was of timbers
Hewn from the cypress-tree, and carefully fitted
    together.
Large and low was the roof; and on slender columns
    supported,
Rose-wreathed, vine-encircled, a broad and spacious
    verandah,
Haunt of the humming-bird and the bee, extended
    around it."

Mr. Lynton had been settled in this house
in the woods for many years. It was the
birthplace of all his children; and though
most of them were now married and had
homes of their own, they all loved to revisit
the dear old house where they had spent
the happy days of their youth.   Harry, the
youngest, was the last chick left in the nest;
and he was not a whit behind the others in
his affection for his beautiful home.

Mr. and Mrs. Lynton were well known
and highly esteemed in all the country
round; and before the neighbourhood had
attracted so many settlers, Mr. Lynton had
acted for many years as clergyman, lawyer,
and doctor to the whole district.   He was a
good naturalist too, and the hall at Lyntonville was full of curiosities, and was famous
in that part of Canada as a museum of
natural objects.   Harry Lynton inherited his
father's tastes; and it was his great delight
to discover a rare insect, or bird, or flower,

which might be added to its treasures. This hall was a large, square room, into which the front door opened; it had been originally intended (Canadian fashion) for a parlour. Several other apartments surrounded it, and opposite the entrance was a large open fireplace, where the great logs were piled in winter, and blazed away cheerily up the wide chimney. A deer-skin lay in front for a rug, and several stag's heads, arranged according to their ages by the branching ntlers, looked down from the wall over the c k n mantelpiece. Large cases of bright-co d birds were there, all of which Mr. Lynto. ad himself shot; aye, and stuffed, too, with his own hands. In one corner was a cabinet of butterflies, moths, and beetles; in another, a bristling porcu pine stood in an attitude of defiance. Here, a racoon curled himself up in close imitation of life; and there, a snarling wolf showed his cruel white teeth. Spreading fungi stood out like huge brackets from the wall—in short, it were vain to attempt to enumerate all the wonders that were there. In the long winter evenings, especially about Christmastide, when the children used to gather around the great hall fire, and ask "grandpapa" for one of his marvellous hunting-stories, the little ones would cast furtive and fearful glances at the wild animals, which seemed so lifelike in the flickering firelight; or would look round, half expecting to hear the wild war-whoop issue from the hollow garments of the Indian chief in the shadowy background.

But there were even greater attractions for Harry out of doors. A swift-running river rippled and splashed all day long at the foot of the sloping ground on which the house was built, and was the source of endless fun and adventure. Boating, bathing, fishing, and hunting for crawfish in their hiding places under the stones, were never-failing amusements in summer; and when the bright waters were ice-bound, his skates and his sledge were in constant requisition. At the time our story begins, the ice had not long broken up, and this year it had been unusually grand. The great blocks upheaved with loud explosions, and groaned and creaked as they were jammed together into huge masses near the bridge, which was partially torn away and carried down the stream by the tremendous force of the pressure. It was a magnificent sight, though the damage caused by the floating ice was very great. In a little cottage, just across the river, lived Philip Quin, with his widowed mother. He was Harry's schoolfellow and inseparable companion. He was a pale, delicate boy, with brown hair and dark blue eyes; sensitive and shy in disposition, and very prone to spend more time over his books than his weakly constitution would allow. Harry, on the contrary, was fair-haired, tall, and robust; but he was not so studiously inclined as to be in any danger of impairing his health. The two boys were certainly very different, but such firm friends that one seemed scarcely happy without the other. Let us now follow them down to the bridge, where they are busy picking up the bits of wood old Michael Lockyer casts aside in his work of repair.

"I say, Mike," said Harry, "tell us what this place was like when you first came to live here."

The old man looked up. "Aye, Master Lynton, I've nigh forgot what them days wor like, by now; but one thing I know, it wasn't like it is at the present, hereaway. Why, the woods came down thick to the water's edge, and ne'er a house nor yet a shanty stood up there where Lyntonville is now; and yet that's old, as we count it, for it's a matter o' fifty year since the first log was laid."

"I suppose there were lots of wolves and

bears and things about here then?" said
Harry : " You must have had many a brush
with them in your time, Mike. Tell us about
one, like a good old fellow—now do ! I know
you can."

" Or about the beavers," interposed Philip.

" Yes ! yes ! the beavers. Oh ! do, Mike.
I've heard you say before you had seen
them."

" Well, well, lads, I'll tell ye what I can ;
but ye must let me get on with my work, or
I shan't be done by nightfall. What was it
I was going to tell ye ?—ah ! the beavers, so
it was. I don't know as how I ever had
much to do with 'em, though. Do ye see
that 'ere stump down there ? Well, that
were some o' their doin's ! "

" What ! the beaver's?" exclaimed Philip ;
" why they never could have cut off such a
tree as that ! "

" Aye, but they could, though ; and those
marks are nothing more nor less than the
nibbles o' their sharp teeth, I can tell ye,"
said Mike.

" But did you ever see them ? " asked
Harry.

" Why yes, to be sure, many a time when
I was a little chap. I used to come about
here with my father when he went hunting.

then ?" said
many a brush
Tell us about
w do! I know

rposed Philip.
)h ! do, Mike.
ou had seen

) what I can;
i my work, or
What was it
he beavers, so
y I ever had
. Do ye see
Well, that

iimed Philip;
it off such a

i; and those
ess than the
can tell ye,"

em ?" asked

a time when
come about
ent hunting.

It's sixty year agone or more since I first set eyes on that 'ere beaver lodge, and now there aint so much as a stick left. We lived a good bit away then, so 'twas a long trudge, and right glad was I to hear the noise of the fall down yonder. By-and-by my father says to me, 'Now, Mike, you stand behind this tree and keep quiet, or you won't have a chance to see 'em.' Well, I looked, and there was the river dammed up into a kind of pond like, with stakes driven into the water, and wattled with twigs like hurdles, and the holes filled in with clay to make all tight, and round the edge were ten or a dozen queer-looking mud huts, but ne'er a beaver did I see. 'Father,' says I, 'where are they ?' ''Bide still,' says he, 'or you'll see naught !' So I watched, and after a bit a brown head popped up, and looked all around, and down he went again. Then four or five came out of the huts, and seemed to listen; and presently one of 'em gave a slap with his big, flat tail, and they all set to work mending a bit of the dam that was broken down."

"Oh ! Mike, I can't believe it," cried Harry.

"Aye, but they did, though," said Mike, "and it was wonderful, surely, to see 'em. If they'd been masons they couldn't h ' done

B

their work better; and how I did laugh
to myself, to be sure, to see one of 'em
carrying the mortar on his tail, and plasterin'
up the wall as if he'd been all his life a
'prentice to the trade! There was one big
fellow who seemed to be 'boss,'* for when-
ever he slapped his tail, some of 'em went to
do his bidding. After we'd stood and looked
at 'em a while, my father says to me, 'Now
Mike, we'll go home; and don't you forget
the beavers, for there's many a lesson you
may learn from 'em.' 'No, father,' says I,
'for I shall know now what you mean when
you say, "as busy as a beaver."' There's
none of 'em left now," added the old man, as
he took up his axe again, "for even then the
trappers had found 'em out, and took a good
many every year, for the sake of their pelt, and
their tails—which are reckoned very good
eating; and after a while the rest took fright,
and forsook the dam."

"I'll tell you what," said Harry, "I'll
ask papa to tell us more about them; and
perhaps some day he may take us up the
river far enough to find a beaver dam."

"I guess you'd have to go a goodish number of miles afore you came across one then,"
said Mike; "but it's getting late, and it's

* *i.e.*, master.

time for me to leave work—and so, my lads,
I'll wish you a very good night."*

* It may be here observed that the beaver and
the maple-leaf are the national emblems of the
Canadas, and none more suitable could have been
chosen; for the beaver speaks of unwearied diligence,
while the maple-leaf represents the vast sources of
wealth which the country affords—the maple being
one of the most valuable of North American trees.
Should any of our young readers be stamp collectors,
and have been fortunate enough to obtain a local
Canadian threepenny stamp, they will find on it the
same design. Our brothers on the other side of the
wide Atlantic, therefore, are in little danger of for-
getting (from this daily reminder) that patient
industry on their part is needful, before their adopted
country will yield to them her boundless treasures of
the forest and the field.

CHAPTER II.

THE LONG CROSS SCHOOL.

" From the neighbouring school come the boys,
With more than their wouted noise
And commotion."

ABOUT two miles and a half from Lyntonville was the small village of Fairfield, con-
sisting chiefly of one principal street which
led straight across the bridge and up the high
bank of the river; while two rival mills and
a few frame houses and shanties, dotted here
and there on the opposite side, comprised the
whole of the settlement. Standing a short
distance back from the top of the steep village
street, was the little wooden church. It was
surrounded by a dark background of pine-
trees, which rocked and swayed in the breeze,
close by the quiet churchyard, where many
a settler from the surrounding country had
already been laid to rest. Still farther away,
to the right, was the Long Cross School—a
low, rough building, with shingled roof, and
wooden walls grown grey by long exposure to

)

wind and weather. It derived its name from
being situated on the Cross-road, leading
through a large cedar swamp, which connected
the woods of Lyntonville with those of Fairfield. Had you peeped in at the door, you
would have seen boys of all sorts and sizes,
rich and poor, at the Long Cross School, for
there was no other for many miles round.
John and Charlie Redfern, the clergyman's
sons; Tom Hardy, from the dry goods
store at the corner; and Philip Quin, were
all in the same class with Harry Lynton and
several others; and we shall become better
acquainted with some of them before our
story is finished.

One fine spring morning, Harry was
walking leisurely to school, swinging his
books by the leathern strap that bound them,
when his quick eye spied a flying-squirrel,
leaping from bough to bough in a large rock-
elm close to the path. Immediately he gave
chase, and after a long and exciting scramble,
which led him far out of his road, he succeeded in securing it under his cap; and then
he hurried on, eager to show his prize to his
schoolfellows. What was his dismay when
he found the door closed, and heard through
the open window the busy hum of the boys'
voices repeating their lessons. There was no

help for it now, however, so he tried to slip in
quietly unobserved.   A class was just going
up, and Harry thought he had escaped notice ;
but unfortunately it was by no means the
first offence.

"I say, won't you catch it for being late
again!" whispered his next neighbour. "Old
Elmslie has been asking for you."

"Can't be helped," said Harry.   "I've
caught a flying-squirrel!"

"Oh! do let us see it, Lynton!" said
Charlie Redfern, "where is it?"

"It's in my pocket; I can't show it you
now. It will be off, if I don't take care."

"I say, what's the fun?" telegraphed
another from an opposite form.   Harry drew
a rough sketch on his slate and held it
up.

"Silence, there!" cried Mr. Elmslie from
his desk, and instantly the boys were as still
as mice.   But Harry could think of nothing
but his squirrel, which was bobbing about in
his pocket, as if it would break bounds every
moment.   Soon the fifth form was called up ;
but not one word of his lesson could Harry
remember, for the squirrel was still upper-
most in his mind.   "I say, Phil, do you
think it will eat it's way out?" he whispered.

" What ? " said Philip, who knew nothing about it.

" I've got a flying-squirrel in my pocket. I caught it coming to school ! "

" You'd better not bother about it now, you'll lose your place if you don't mind."

"Lynton," said the master, " you know the rules ; go to the foot of the class, and don't let me have to speak to you again."

Harry tried to attend for a few minutes ; then it struck him that the squirrel had been very still for a long time ; could it be dead ? He could not resist the temptation of putting his hand very gently into his pocket to see if all was right. Hardly had he done so, when a bite, sharp enough to draw blood, made him hastily withdraw it, and the little prisoner, taking advantage of the opening, sprang out of his pocket, and leaped first on the master's desk, where it upset the ink all over his books and papers—then settled on little Percy Hamilton's curly head, entangling its claws in his long hair—then freeing itself with a struggle and a bound, it cleared the open window, and was off to the shelter of its native woods, well pleased no doubt to be let out of school ! The boys shouted ; those who were in the secret laughing heartily at poor Harry's misfortune, while the others,

completely mystified at the sudden commotion,
asked each other what it all meant.   Even
Mr. Elmslie's voice failed in quieting them
for some moments ; but order being at length
restored, Harry was told to stand out.

"Now, sir," said the master, "what am I
to say to you for causing all this damage and
disturbance?"

Harry stood silent, and the matter ended
by his having to spend that long, bright half-
holiday alone in the Long Cross School, with
all his lessons to learn over again, and a long
imposition besides.   But although Harry was
inclined to be idle sometimes, he had nevertheless many good points in his character.
He was open-hearted and generous ; and in
any case of oppression or wrong-doing
amongst his school-fellows, he was sure to
stand up for the right.

It so happened that when Philip Quin
first joined the school, he incurred the dislike
of Tom Hardy, one of the biggest and most
unpopular of the boys.   For a long time,
Hardy, who was not wanting in quickness and
ability, had been considered head of the fifth,
or highest form ; but he took advantage of
his standing to bully his companions.   Very
soon after Philip joined, however, Hardy
found his position becoming more and more

untenable every day, and before many weeks had passed he was completely deposed. In consequence, Hardy lost no opportunity of annoying and holding him up to ridicule, on the score of his poverty, which was only too plainly betrayed by his patched and threadbare coat. One day Hardy was more than usually coarse and rude in his conduct to Philip in the playground, who bore his "chaff" very meekly, though his pale face glowed with the bright flush of suppressed feeling. Presently Harry was attracted by the loud tones of Hardy's voice, and though he did not know much of Philip at that time he could not calmly see the weak oppressed.

"Come now, Hardy, you just stop that, will you," said he; "I'm not going to stand it."

"Then just take yourself off, and leave me to mind my own business," said Hardy. "If you don't look out I'll pitch into you, my boy."

Some of the lads burst out laughing at this speech, for they all knew that Hardy's words were much more valiant than his deeds.

"Come on then!" said Harry, "let's have it out, for you shan't bother Quin any more if I can help it."

"Oh, don't, Lynton, pray don't fight on my account; what he says does me no harm, and

I don't mind; please don't!" and Philip
looked distressed. By this time, however,
Harry's coat was off, and a ring of boys had
gathered round the combatants—most of them
rallying round Harry, though one or two sided
with his opponent. Hardy, like most bullies,
was a sad coward, and he was rather frightened
when he saw the turn affairs had taken; but he
felt that if he showed the white feather now, he
would lose his position in the playground as
well as in his class, so with a great deal of
bluster he prepared to fight his young anta-
gonist. Several blows were struck on both
sides, and Harry succeeded in punishing Hardy
severely, though a bruised face and black
eye proved that he himself had not escaped
in defending the weak. At this moment
Mr. Elmslie rather unexpectedly made his
appearance.

"Now, boys, what's all this about?" said
he, very gravely. "Go, Lynton, and wash
your face, and then come into school, where
I will speak to you, which I cannot do in your
present state." Harry walked off, looking
very deplorable.

"Who was the other?" continued Mr.
Elmslie, looking round, but Hardy had contrived to slip off unobserved, and was not
to be seen.

"If you please, sir," said Philip, coming forward and speaking very earnestly, "don't blame Lynton, for he did it out of kindness; indeed he did, sir, though I begged him not."

"A strange way of showing kindness, truly! And are you mixed up in this affair, too, Quin? I should not have believed it possible," said Mr. Elmslie, in evident displeasure.

Philip coloured, and did not know what to say, for he could not bear his friend to suffer unjustly, while he did not like to allude to Hardy's provoking and unkind taunts about his poverty. He stood silent for a moment, and then said, very respectfully, "If you please, sir, may I explain? Hardy was teasing me, and Harry took my part, which led to the fight."

"There seems to have been very small provocation, Quin; and as I entirely disapprove of the practice, I shall certainly make examples of Lynton and Hardy."

"Oh, sir!" cried Charlie Redfern, a bright little fellow of eleven, who was never afraid of speaking his mind; "oh, Mr. Elmslie, it wouldn't be fair, indeed it wouldn't. Hardy is a big bully, and he is always going on at Quin about being poor, and I don't know what all. It's more than any fellow can stand,

sir ; and it's all because he takes him down
in school.   It's a downright shame the way
he goes on, and Lynton said he wouldn't stand
it any longer, for Quin bears it so meekly and
never says a word.   It's Hardy that's to blame
if any one is; you would have thought so yourself, sir, if you had been here."   And he
stopped, breathless with his long speech.

"Is this the case, boys?"

"Yes, sir!" "It is really, sir!" cried several
voices together.

"Well, then," said Mr. Elmslie, as Harry
reappeared, "that alters the case.   I am
glad to find, Lynton, that you are not so much
to blame in this matter as I imagined at
first ; but, boys, I wish I could teach you to
remember that this is not the way to settle
disputes, or make wrong come right.   I am
very thankful, Quin, to find that you do not
harbour illwill, or desire to resent an injury.
I trust the disposition to bear meekly with
insults proceeds from a truly noble effort on
your part, my boy," and Mr. Elmslie looked
kindly at Philip ; " I mean, an effort to follow
in the steps of Him who was meek and lowly
in heart, and forgave every trespass.   As for
Hardy, he must be differently dealt with."

rdy that's to blame
c thought so your-
here." And he
i long speech.
.,

sir!" cried several

Elmslie, as Harry
the case. I am
ou are not so much
as I imagined at
:ould teach you to
the way to settle
ime right. I am
d that you do not
resent an injury.
bear meekly with
ily noble effort on
r. Elmslie looked
an effort to follow
is meek and lowly
trespass. As for
ily dealt with."

CHAPTER III.

SIGHTS IN THE WOOD.

" There's not a leaf within the bower,
  There's not a bird upon the tree,
There's not a dew-drop on the flower,
  But bears the impress, Lord, of Thee.
Yes, dew-drops, leaves, and birds, and all
  The smallest like the greatest things,
The sea's vast space, the earth's wide ball,
  Alike proclaim Thee King of kings."

From the day of the fight, Harry and Philip
had been fast friends, and many a pleasant
expedition they had together. Harry's open,
fearless character had a good influence
upon Philip, who was timid and sensitive;
while Philip's high principles and thoughtful
piety were a check upon Harry's natural
heedlessness. One Saturday, being a holiday,
Harry ran off as usual to seek his friend, and
when he reached the cottage he found him
sitting in an arbour in the garden reading.
This little retreat was the work of Philip's
own hands, and he had spent many busy
hours in its construction. He could even
tell the spot where each knotted stick and

c

fir-cone and curious pebble had been found.
When at length the last nail was driven in,
and he had really completed his long-
cherished design, his delight was great, and
he was proud indeed when his mother
promised to honour his little edifice by drink-
ing tea there with him the first evening after
it was finished. Harry's emulation had been
roused by the successful labours of his companion, and he too had attempted something
of the same kind; but he soon became weary
of his work, and gave it up, like many other
things which he had thrown aside in the same
way.

Philip looked up as Harry's shadow fell
on his open book.

" Oh, Harry," said he, "are you going for
a walk?"

" Yes," cried Harry, "come along; it's
so jolly in the woods to-day, and we shall
find ever so many things!"

Philip went in to tell his mother, and then
joined his friend, and the two lads set off
together. The woods certainly were very
inviting, for flowers of every hue sprang up
at their feet, and every little hillock was
carpeted with soft mosses and crowned with
the delicate fronds of the oak-fern, or the
glossy black stems of the maiden-hair.

had been found.
l was driven in,
cted his long-
was great, and
n his mother
edifice by drink-
rst evening after
ulation had been
urs of his com-
pted something
n became weary
ike many other
side in the same

y's shadow fell

e you going for

me along; it's
and we shall

other, and then
vo lads set off
nly were very
hue sprang up
le hillock was
l crowned with
ık-fern, or the
maiden-hair.

Large lily-like plants,* called by the Indians "deaths," on account of the deadly poison which lurks beneath their fair appearance, nodded their beautiful snowy or chocolate-coloured blossoms in the breeze. The sunlight shimmered and glanced through the waving boughs, brightening the little nooks and dells, here flecking the sober pines with its golden gleam, there kissing the ripe red strawberries scattered in abundance over the ground. But amidst all these beauties Philip looked grave and out of spirits; and at length he said, "It was this day three years ago that my father died."

"Do you remember him?" asked Harry.

"Oh, yes! quite well. I was ten then; and we had just come over from Ireland, mamma, and papa, and Edith—that was my little sister, and our old nurse, Norah. I remember so well the day we arrived at Montreal seeing the squaws come on board ship with their baskets and moccasins for sale. I was frightened, rather, and so was Edie, until mamma told us all about them. Well, we stayed there some time, and then papa heard of a farm that would suit him, and it was while we were on our journey to the place (I forget the name), that papa was taken

* Trillium.

ill of cholera and died. Then Edie took it,
and old Norah, and they were all buried in
the same grave."

"Oh Philip! how dreadful."

"Yes," said Philip, "it was a dreadful
time. And afterwards mamma was very ill;
and when she got better we came here. I
remember Edie and I had ponies in Ireland,
and we used to ride with papa very often. I
never had a shabby coat then;" and Philip
looked down at his well-worn sleeves, patched
in more than one place—"but that doesn't
matter," he added, hastily, "it is mamma
that I care about. If I were only a man I
could earn something to make her more
comfortable."

"Well," said Harry, "you are so clever
that you will be able to do it some day. It's
my belief you could teach a school as well as
Mr. Elmslie now."

Thus chatting together, Philip became
more cheerful, and the two boys kept along
the edge of the forest for some distance,
gathering the strawberries and filling their
hands with the different wild flowers that
tempted them on at every step.

"I say, look here!" said Harry, "the
mandrakes are out!" and he lifted one of
the broad twin-leaves of a curious-looking

Edie took it,
all buried in

as a dreadful
was very ill;
me here. I
es in Ireland,
ery often. I
' and Philip
eves, patched
that doesn't
is mamma
nly a man I
e her more

e so clever
o day. It's
l as well as

lip became
kept along
e distance,
lling their
owers that

rry, "the
ed one of
us-looking

plant, and showed Philip a large white waxen flower, like a wild rose, growing close to the foot-stalk, which had been hidden from sight. " We must mark the place and come here when the fruit is ripe."

" What is it like?" said Philip.

" It is about the size of an egg, and has a thick yellow skin, with seeds like a gooseberry. It's first-rate, I can tell you. Suppose we go farther into the wood now, we shan't find much more out here."

" What's this?" said Philip, as he stooped to pick up something that looked like a tobacco-pipe curiously carved in wax, stuck into the ground bowl upwards, at the foot of a pine.

" Oh, I'm so glad you've found one!" cried Harry, " it must be the 'Indian pipe' old Mike told me about. I believe it's nothing but a fungus; see, it's turning black already. Didn't it look just as if someone had put it there and forgotten it?"*

" Oh, did you see that bird?" exclaimed Philip, abruptly, " it was bright scarlet, and passed like a flash of fire!"

" It's a tannager, but it is not all scarlet; it has black wings, I know, because papa has

---

* Monotropa.

c 2

one stuffed.   Yes, there he goes ! and
there's a blue jay !   Hark ! do you hear his
scream ? "

And so, attracted by one strange sight
after another, the boys wandered on, deeper
and deeper into the forest, until at last Philip
said, " Don't you think we ought to be going
home, Harry?   It must be getting late."

They had left the little wood path a long
while before to pick a flower here, and to get
a glimpse of a squirrel or bright bird there ;
and now, when it was time for them to retrace
their steps, they could not remember in
which direction they had come.   Above and
around them were thick tall trees—so tall
that they could only catch a glimpse of the
sky now and then—and not a sign of foot-
path could they see.   Their feet sank deep
into the rich soft mould, formed by the
fallen leaves for hundreds of years, and it
seemed as if no other footstep had ever passed
that way.   The two boys stood still for a
moment and consulted.

" Here's a pretty go ! " said Harry ; " I'm
sure I don't remember which way we came,
do you ?"

" No," said Philip, looking very much
frightened ; " the trees are all alike, and
there's no path.   What shall we do, Harry ?"

io goes ! and
lo you hear his

strange sight
red on, deeper
il at last Philip
ght to be going
ting late."
d path a long
re, and to get
t bird there;
hem to retrace
remember in
. Above and
rees—so tall
impse of the
sign of foot-
et sank deep
med by the
·ears, and it
l ever passed
still for a

arry; "I'm
y we came,

very much
alike, and
o, Harry?"

"Oh, never mind; we'll soon find it. I think it was this way,—we'll try it, at any rate."

They turned in the direction he indicated, and walked on for some distance without speaking.

"Do you remember that fallen tree, Harry?" said Quin, as they came to a large trunk completely uprooted, lying all across their path.

"I can't say I do, Philip. I'm afraid we're wrong after all; we must go back."

Again they turned, and as they went, the undergrowth seemed to become thicker, as it brushed past their faces and scratched and tore their clothes, which made them think they were going farther and farther into the wood. Up and down they wandered; Harry saying all he could think of to keep up poor Philip's courage, though it must be confessed his own was fast oozing away, for the time was passing on. It was getting dark, as the sun had nearly set. They felt that the blackness of night would soon be upon them, and they were alone in the great silent forest. Philip held Harry's hand tightly clasped in his own, and they looked at each other without speaking a word. Just then, a large bird flew up, and startled them with its heavy flight, and all was still again—so still, that they could almost hear their hearts beating.

" Oh, Harry," said Philip, at last, " what will my mother do when she finds we don't come back? Do you think we shall ever find our way back?"

" I don't know," said Harry, " perhaps they'll look for us; but I'm afraid they don't know which way we went. I wonder if any one would hear if we shouted?"

Again and again they shouted, but the sound only waked the echoes of the forest, and startled one or two birds that had gone to roost in the trees near; so they gave it up in despair.

Presently Harry said, " Philip, let us kneel down and say our prayers—perhaps God will help us."

They knelt down hand in hand at the foot of a tree, and Philip uttered a few words of earnest prayer, that God would take care of them and bring them back safely to their homes. When they rose from their knees, Philip said, " Do you remember the psalm, Harry, ' Thou compassest my path and my lying down, and art acquainted with all my ways. The night shineth as the day: the darkness and the light are both alike to thee.' I don't think we ought to be afraid.

-so still, that
arts beating.
last, "what
nds we don't
ve shall ever

y, "perhaps
id they don't
vonder if any

ed, but the
f the forest,
t had gone to
gave it up

ilip, let us
rs—perhaps

at the foot
w words of
ake care of
ly to their
icir knees,
the psalm,
h and my
th all my
day: the
a alike to
be afraid.

for God is with us here just as much as if we
were at home."

"But, Philip, suppose we are starved to
death!"

"Oh, but Harry, we've asked God to take
care of us; and I know He will, because
He has promised to hear our prayers, for
Christ's sake."

The two boys began to feel less hopeless,
as, comforting each other, they thus remembered that their Father in heaven was
near, however far they might be from their
earthly parents' aid.

CHAPTER IV.

A NIGHT IN THE FOREST.

"Abide with me, fast falls the eventide,
 The darkness thickens ; Lord, with me abide.
 When other helpers fail, and comforts flee,
 Help of the helpless, oh ! abide with me."

"I wish we could light a fire, Harry, it's getting very dark, and I'm so cold."

"Ah ! that's a capital idea, and I believe we can do it, too, for I've got the matches in my pocket that we were going to use when we fired off the cannon yesterday."

They set to work and gathered a large heap of dry wood, which, after many failures, they managed to light with some dead leaves, and soon it burned up brightly. The fire was a great comfort, and afforded them some occupation as well, for they employed all the little light that was left in making a pile of sticks to keep it up all night. This done, they sat down by it, and tried to make themselves as comfortable as they could under the circumstances. It was now quite dark, and

REST.

ntide,
ith me abide.
nforts flee,
with me."

e, Harry, it's
old."
and I believe
he matches in
o use when we

hered a large
many failures,
he dead leaves,
ly. The fire
ed them some
ployed all the
king a pile of
his done, they
ke themselves
l under the
ite dark, and

A NIGHT IN THE FOREST.

33

they talked as much as possible, for the dead silence was more than they could bear. Now and then the dry wood crackled and flared up, and as soon as the flame died away, they piled on more fuel to keep up a blaze. Sleep, of course, was out of the question, and they sat there listening to every little sound and conjuring up all sorts of terrors, both real and imaginary. The rustle of a dead leaf was enough to make them start; and once, when a wild unearthly scream broke the stillness of the night, just above their heads, they clung to each other in terrible fear, until they heard the heavy flapping of wings, and remembered it could be nothing but an owl in search of its prey. Slowly and wearily passed the time; each moment seemed an hour to their excited fancy, but as the night wore on they became more calm, and Harry had nearly regained his wonted courage, when they heard a heavy, crashing sound, as of some large animal coming through the brushwood! Nearer and nearer it approached, and their hearts died within them; they hardly dared to breathe lest the sound should attract the attention of the beast. They each caught up a lighted brand from the fire as the only weapon within reach, and put themselves in

an attitude of defence. Presently the bushes
on the other side of the fire parted—they
saw two red eye-balls glaring at them, and
could just distinguish the huge outlines of a
bear through the gloom ! There it stood for
some time, evidently not knowing what to
make of the unwonted sight of a fiery pile in
its hitherto undisturbed haunts,—and there
stood the boys, motionless, their eyes fixed
on the unwelcome invader of their solitude.
After a while, it gave a low growl, and
raising its head snuffed about as if in search
of them ; but at that moment, the fire which
was getting low, fell in, and a bright blaze
shot up, crackling and sparkling as it rose.
This seemed to alarm the bear, which is well
known to be a cowardly animal, unless
suffering from extreme hunger. It turned
with a parting grunt, and slowly trotted off ;
and they heard its retreating footsteps
growing fainter and more faint in the distance ! After this they had no further
alarms, but the time seemed to pass more
tediously than ever, for they feared lest their
dreaded enemy should return again. Most
thankful were they, when the first pale
streaks of dawning light told them that
morning was near, and that the long horrible
darkness was past.

"It's Sunday morning, Philip," said Harry.

"Yes," whispered Philip, we ought to thank God," and once again they knelt to render their heartfelt praise for their preservation from the dangers of the night.

At length, when it was light enough for them to see each other distinctly, Harry was startled to observe how haggard poor Philip looked. He was not a strong boy at any time, and want of food for so many hours, combined with the terrors of their situation, had been too much for him; but he said nothing, and they began to look about for wild berries to satisfy their hunger. They could find nothing, however, but a few plants of the Indian turnip—a kind of arum—not unlike our English "lords and ladies."

"Do you know, Philip," said Harry, "I've heard that the Indians eat these roots, but if they are not cooked in one particular way, they hurt one's throat and mouth most fearfully. I believe they roast them,—shall we try? We shall starve if we don't eat something, and there are no berries about here."

"Yes, perhaps it would be a good plan," said Philip, "but I can't say I feel very hungry."

Harry pulled up some of the roots and washed them in a little stream hard by; then covering them with the hot wood embers, he piled on more sticks and left them to roast themselves. "What had we better do?" said he; "shall we try again to find our way back? If we could only get to the river, we should be all right. You know we could notch the trees, so that we might find the fire again."

Philip agreed to this proposal, but Harry was shocked to see him sink back in a kind of faint as he tried to rise.

"Oh! Philip, dear Philip, what is the matter? What shall I do if you are ill? Stay, I'll get some water;" and hurrying down to the tiny stream, he soon came back with some in his cap, and kneeling down he began to bathe Philip's face. It was some time before he opened his eyes.

"There, that's right, old fellow! you'll be better directly. It's because we have not eaten anything for so long," said Harry. "I feel very queer too. But how cold you are!" And in a moment his coat was off, and he was wrapping it round his friend.

"Hark! I heard a shout, I am certain I did!" cried he, joyfully. They listened intently, and again the welcome sound broke upon their ears. Harry shouted with all his might; and then, to their intense joy, they heard footsteps approaching, and presently the friendly dusky face of old Peter Muskrat, an Indian well known in the neighbourhood, appeared through the trees. Over his shoulder was slung a fawn, and the string of black bass* in his hand showed he had been on a foraging expedition. Indeed, so good a hunter was he, that Mr. Lynton was accustomed to take him as a guide in his autumn hunting excursions. The boys made him understand that they had lost their way, and asked him to help them.

"Ugh! Lynton good man," said he; "take boys home,—give Peter blanket-coat for winter! Come—squaw give food—wigwam not far off." Then seeing Philip looked pale and weak, he produced a flask from a sort of birch-bark knapsack, and made him swallow a mouthful of something which took away his breath, and proved to be whisky. It did him good, however; but as he still lagged behind, old Peter took him up in his strong arms and carried him, while Harry followed with some of the Indian's spoils. After a while they began to hear the roar of the river, and a turn in the path brought them

* Fish commonly found in the lakes and rivers of Canada.

D 2

in sight of the Indian camp. It consisted of
a few tent-like wigwams ; and at the doors,
or rather entrances of two or three of them,
sat several squaws—some making baskets to
sell in the neighbouring villages, and others
engaged in ornamenting their deerskin moccasins with bright coloured beads. They all
wore the embroidered leggings and moccasins
of their tribe, but the rest of their costume
was a motley mixture of civilized attire and
their own native garments. One old squaw,
who proved to be Mrs. Muskrat, was watching a huge pot, hung over a wood fire by
means of stakes driven into the ground, the
contents of which she stirred now and then
with a stick. Old Peter threw down the
fawn and the fish at the door of his wigwam,
and, speaking to his wife in their own lan-
guage, they conferred together for some
minutes. The boys could not help laughing
at some of the little baby Indians—papooses
as they called them—which were bound in tight
swathing bands to a flat piece of birch-bark,
and were hung up in any available situation,
whence they peered about with their round
black eyes. "They are just like the tails of
Bo-peep's sheep," said Harry, "all hung on
a tree to dry!" By this time several more
men made their appearance, but took very

little notice of the boys beyond the customary "Ugh!" and a shrug of their broad shoulders. Presently the old squaw turning out the contents of the great pot into a sort of wooden bowl or platter, they gathered round it, helping themselves with their fingers, while the women kept at a respectful distance. Peter gave the two boys some of this savoury dish in a smaller bowl, and though they wondered what they were eating they were too hungry to be very fastidious, and Harry at least did ample justice to the meal. "I shouldn't be surprised if this were bull-frog stew," said he to Philip; "I know these fellows eat them, and the little bones look very suspicious. However I shan't ask any questions; I never was so hungry in all my life."

"I wonder, whether they will show us the way home soon," said Philip, who seemed more anxious for that than for anything else, "and whether anyone has been looking for us?" By this time they had finished, and old Muskrat brought them the bottle, which had been passing pretty freely from mouth to mouth, but the boys shook their heads. "No?" said he, in surprise, " leetle boys not know what's good!" then putting it to his own mouth, he tossed off their share as if it were so much water.

"Peter's squaw show way—Lynton give blanket-coat," said he, as the old woman came out of her wigwam, baskets in hand, in hopes of getting customers at Lyntonville. "Yes, yes!" said Harry, much amused at his anxiety to be paid for his trouble; taking a penknife, which happened to be nearly new, out of his pocket he gave it to the old man, who grinned with delight. They then bade adieu to the friendly Indians, and with a last look at the funny little papooses, they followed the Indian along the banks of the river, and were amazed to find how soon they reached their own familiar haunts.

When they came in sight of the house Harry threw up his cap, and shouted "hurrah" at the top of his voice. The two mothers, who were together, heard the welcome sound, and hardly daring to believe that their ears had not deceived them, rushed into the verandah, and in a few moments the boys were clasped in their arms. "My dear, dear boys!" said Mrs. Lynton, "thank God, we have you safe again! Where have you been? Your father, Harry, and the neighbours have been out all night searching for you." Numberless were the questions that poured in upon them; and meanwhile the old squaw stood with characteristic patience awaiting their leisure, for she had no idea of departing without a gift of some sort. She was liberally rewarded, and obtained a promise of the blanket-coat upon which old Peter seemed to have set his heart. A meal was also provided for her, and to the boys' astonishment she not only managed to dispose of a large portion of a round of beef, but stowed away the remainder in her basket, as well as the rest of a loaf of goodly size which had been placed before her. The boys were not aware that Indian etiquette obliged her to do this—as to leave any food put before them on the table would be considered a breach of good manners.

CHAPTER V.

" 'Tis not the eye of keenest blaze,
  Nor the quick swelling breast,
That soonest thrills at touch of praise—
  These do not please Him best."

IT was too late to attend the morning service,
which must have been already begun ere they
reached their home, and the boys were glad
to rest awhile after their long walk and sleep-
less night; but in the afternoon, the whole
party set out for the little church at Fairfield.
As they approached the bell began to ring,
and Philip thought he had never heard music
so sweet as that which called the worshippers
together to the house of God.   They entered
the church with hearts thankful that they
were once more permitted to engage all together in the service of the sanctuary.
Earnestly they joined in the prayers and
praises which were offered, and when Mr.
Redfern, the minister, went into the pulpit
and gave out his text, Harry and Philip were

struck with the singular appropriateness of the passage. It was this—" Oh that men would praise the Lord for his goodness, and for his wonderful works to the children of men " (Psa. cvii. 8). They listened still more attentively when the preacher referred to the verses preceding it—" They wandered in the wilderness in a solitary way; they found no city to dwell in. Hungry and thirsty, their soul fainted within them. Then they cried unto the Lord in their trouble, and he delivered them out of their distresses. And he led them forth by a right way, that they might go to a city of habitation."

" My brethren," said the good man, " who is there amongst us that cannot testify to the goodness of the Lord? Who cannot point at some time or other of their lives to some special deliverance—some danger averted, or life spared, when no human arm was near to aid, no human voice to comfort and assure? Aye, and when the cry for help and deliverance from the threatened danger has been wrung from a full heart, has it no* many a time been coupled with a vow, that once free —once escaped—the spared life should be devoted to the service of the Strong Deliverer? If any such are here, let me urge them to remember that hour, and to pay unto the

Lord these solemn vows. But while we consider these verses in their literal meaning, we must not forget that there are far greater perils besetting each precious soul, than any that can happen to the body. My friends, have we not all wandered from the strait path? Have we not all strayed into the wilderness of this sinful world, and turned aside from the narrow gate which leadeth unto life? The pleasures of sin have lured us on and on, like the bright flowers by the wayside, until at length our feet begin to stumble upon the slippery paths, and thorns and briers grow up where the fragrant blossoms have been. What a picture is here of the world which lieth in wickedness! Thanks be to God, some amongst us have escaped from its snares, and can now join in the song of the redeemed. But are there none here whose souls are fainting within them because the pleasures have faded, and the troubles and the weariness of sin remain? Oh! my brethren, there is redemption for *you*—there is a city to dwell in prepared for *you*—if you will only seek it in the right way, through the blood and righteousness of our loving Saviour. In Christ there is deliverance; in Christ there is rest; in Christ there is pardon and peace. He is the Door—we must enter by Him. He is the Way—we must follow Him. He is the Rock—we must trust in Him. He is the Life—in Him we have life everlasting.

"Let us ask the aid of His promised Comforter—the Holy Spirit—to teach us all things and testify to us of Him; to work in us the grace of true repentance; to guide us into all truth, and deliver us from all evil. Without the help of the Holy Spirit we can do nothing; but we can never seek His aid in vain, for our Lord himself has said—'If ye then, being evil, know how to give good gifts unto your children, how much more shall your heavenly Father give the Holy Spirit to them that ask him?' (Luke xi. 13.)

"Thus, trusting in Christ alone, and relying on the promised help of His Holy Spirit, we shall be enabled to praise the Lord, not only with our lips but in our lives, walking before him in 'holiness and righteousness all the days of our life.'"

As the boys walked home together after service, Harry looked very grave, and was silent for some time. At length he said, "Oh! Philip, did not the sermon seem like a message to us? I am sure we ought to praise God for being saved from death. When the bear came so close to us last night I

E

prayed to God to deliver us; and I thought if we could only get safe home again, I would be very good, and serve God all my life. But, Philip, it is so hard for us boys to do anything to serve God : if we were men it would be a different thing. I don't see what I can do ' to show forth his praise.' "

" I don't know," said Philip; " but it seems to me that all we can do is to try and do our best in our every-day duties —I mean our lessons, and things ; because I have heard my mother say that God has a work for everyone to do, according to his age and station in life. You remember that verse where St. Paul speaks to servants—' with good will doing service as to the Lord and not to men ; ' well, don't you think if they can serve God in their work, we can, too, in ours, by being steady, and diligent, and obedient, and all that ? "

" I suppose that is the way, Phil ; but I always forget."

" We must ask God to help us, Harry, by his Holy Spirit, for Christ's sake," said Philip.

Philip's advice was remembered, and from this time Harry did become more industrious and painstaking ; and his mother's heart rejoiced when she saw her son striving to do his duty for the Lord's sake.

The two boys were the heroes of the school on the following day, and they had to relate their adventures again and again for the amusement of their companions. The Wednesday after this event had been fixed for the examination and breaking up of the school for the summer vacation. As many parents came on that day to assure themselves of their sons' progress during the past term, the boys always endeavoured to make their school look as festive as possible, by decking it with cedar-boughs and bright flowers. The examination this year was more largely attended than usual; and Mrs. Lynton persuaded Mrs. Quin to join their party, as it was understood that Philip would be declared captain of the school. Some of the parents had subscribed a sum sufficient to enable Mr. Elmslie to give away a few prizes for the encouragement of his scholars, though it was not the usual custom of the school. Great was the excitement, therefore, on the appointed day, for none of the boys knew who would be the fortunate winners of the much-coveted prizes.

The examination was to begin at two o'clock, and before that hour many visitors had arrived. The younger boys (for Mr. Elmslie began with the lower classes) acquitted themselves very fairly, and received a general commendation for diligence in their studies. At length it was the turn of the fifth form to go up, and greater interest began to be shown, as it was to be subjected to a much more difficult examination. Philip, though evidently nervous, passed most creditably, and without a doubt was entitled to hold the first place. Harry, much to his own surprise, ranked second. Poor Hardy, who had hitherto looked upon the examination as his own particular triumph, was completely crestfallen that he was so far down on the list. Philip, therefore, received the prize for general proficiency in school work; and as each class was only entitled to one prize, the others were distributed amongst the younger boys.

When all were given, it was seen that Mr. Elmslie laid a handsomely-bound Bible upon the desk before him, and addressing the boys, he said—"My lads, it has given me much pleasure to distribute among you the prizes which have been kindly placed at my disposal to bestow upon those who deserve encouragement for diligent attention to their studies. Of course, where there are so many competitors, it must necessarily happen that many are disappointed. To these I would say one cheering word—that while *one* in each class has done best, yet there are several who have done well. It is not always the boy who works hardest that wins the prize; for ability and quickness go far to help some, of whose industry I cannot say much. I have therefore made out a list of those in the whole school, whom I find by my books merit special comme dation, which I have now much pleasure in reading." Here followed a long list of names; and many a little boy's eyes sparkled with delight when he heard his own amongst them. Mr. Elmslie at length folded up the paper, and continued—" The prizes which have been bestowed amongst you to-day, are simply intended, as you all know, to testify to your proficiency in the various branches of study in which you are engaged. To the number of these I have added one as a reward for good conduct during the past year, and a token of my own regard for the boy who best deserves it. I have chosen a Bible for this purpose—first, because it is itself the best of all books; and secondly, because it is the best of all guides in enabling those who seek instruction from its pages, to lead a God-fearing, useful, and noble life. I have endeavoured to choose amongst you all as impartially as possible, and I hope when I name Philip Quin as the owner of the book

E 2

I hold in my hand, that my choice will be approved by his companions."

" Hurrah ! yes ! yes ! He is a good fellow ! " cried many voices ; and Philip, with much surprise and a glowing face, went up to the desk to receive the beautiful gift.

" And now, my lads," resumed Mr. Elmslie, " I will not detain you longer than to wish you all a very pleasant holiday ; and may God have us all in his most holy keeping, both now and always."

The boys began to cheer as soon as he had finished, and very soon the books were passing from hand to hand, exciting many remarks and great admiration. Philip found his way at once to his mother's side. Her eyes were full of tears as she whispered a few words of loving approval to her only son, who gave promise of being a real blessing and comfort to his widowed mother. Very soon the school-house was empty, and various groups of the boys and their parents were seen wending their way to their several homes ; and very few carried away with them any other feelings than those of pleasure and satisfaction at the events of the day.

There was one, however, whose face wore a scowl as he met Philip, and in whose heart evil feelings of anger and revenge were

e will bo

a good
ilip, with
went up
rift.
Elmslie,
i to wish
and may
keeping,

s he had
passing
remarks
his way
es were
ords of
10 gavo
comfort
on the
groups
e scen
10mes ;
y other
satis-

wore a
heart
were

burning. This one was Tom Hardy. Never before had an examination passed so much to his disadvantage, and his was not the disposition to bear meekly any fancied wrong. Poor boy ! we must not judge him too harshly, for he had none of the advantages our young friends Harry and Philip possessed. No loving mother had he, to soothe his angry spirit or gently to instil holy principles into his mind ; and his father was a harsh, money-making and money-loving man, with little time and less inclination to train his children in a right way. Tom was reckoned a sharp, clever lad, and Mr. Hardy's friends did not fail to speak honied words of praise of him, too often in his hearing, in order to curry favour with his father, who was looked upon by some of the smaller settlers as a great man in that district. Tom Hardy left the school-house with angry thoughts in his heart, and angry words on his lips. "I'll be even with him yet," said he to himself, "I thought something was in the wind, with his meek religious ways—sneak as he is !—all to get on the right side of old Elmslie; but I'll teach him !" He seemed lost in thought for a while, and then quickening his pace, muttering in a low tone—"That will do ! I've hit it !" he ran down the hill and disappeared.

But what was passing in Philip's mind at
the same time? We fear a humble, lowly
spirit was no longer his—for as he passed
Hardy, his heart glowed with exultation at
his own success, and his feelings were akin to
those of the Pharisee, who dared to thank
God that he was not as other men. Ah!
how short, at any time, is the step between
us and sin ; and what need to pray for God's
preventing grace ! All day he hugged vain
thoughts of his goodness close to his heart,
though none suspected it ; but afterwards
when he knelt down at night, his conscience
smote him as he remembered that his Father
in heaven, " from whom no secrets are hid,"
had read the thoughts of his inmost heart.
A sense of his sin in God's sight weighed
him down, and he whom all had praised that
day, closed it in the secresy of his own little
chamber with the heartfelt prayer, " God be
merciful to me a sinner."

In the meantime, the Lyntonville party, with
the addition of Mrs. Quin, Philip, and Mr.
Elmslie, had reached home ; and the pleasant
day was brought to a close by a row in Mr.
Lynton's large boat on the river. The short
twilight had already begun, but a bright star
twinkled here and there in the dark blue sky,
to light them on their way. There was a

hush in the air which told of the coming
hours of stillness and rest, broken only by
the sighing of the wind in the tree-tops,
mingled with the distant lowing of cattle, or
the loud croak of the bull-frog close at hand.
Fireflies flitted about, gleaming like flashing
emeralds amongst the low bushes by the
water-side; and the plash of the oars kept
time to the evening hymn, begun by Mrs.
Lynton's sweet voice, and sung in chorus by
all the party.   Harry thought he had never
loved their beautiful river so much before;
and he bade his friend " good-night" with un-
mingled happiness, rejoicing in his success.
The dew was falling fast, and the night wind
blew with a chilly breath as they hastened
homewards; but little did any of them dream
of the change that a few short hours would
work on that peaceful scene !

CHAPTER VI.

WHAT CAME OF IT.

" Fire is a good servant, but a bad master."
" Behold how great a matter a little fire kindleth."

HAD any one watched the stealthy footsteps
of a boy who, under the darkening shades of
that summer night, left the village of Fairfield and proceeded in the direction of Mrs.
Quin's cottage, they could hardly have failed
to suspect mischief, and Tom Hardy, for it
was he, might well stop at every sound, and
draw back into deeper shadow. It was but the
wind, however, as it blew back the hair from
his hot forehead, or the echo of his own foot-
fall in the stillness that startled him. His conscience whispered, " Turn back, Tom, turn
back; think what you are going to do;"—but
in vain, Tom would not listen. He tried to
stifle its voice. "It was no such great matter
after all," said he to himself; he was only
going to set fire to Philip's bower; that would
do him no real harm, he might build it again
if he liked. It would but make him angry;

A CRUEL DEED.

and the
the mo
when l
that re
would
discove
good ca
exultan
revenge
By t
all was
and loo
light" t
asleep.
careful
of tarr
rising
loud c
start a
he wer
to his
ing it
which
ing sl
heap.
make
fire, l
were
him

and then what fun it would be to see Philip—
the meek Philip—in a rage, next morning,
when he found a few smouldering ruins, all
that remained of his work! The best of it
would be, too, that no one would be able to
discover the cause of the fire, he would take
good care of that. And Hardy laughed a low
exultant laugh, as he thought over the capital
revenge he had planned.

By this time he had reached the house;
all was still, and he crept round to the back
and looked up at the windows. "There's no
light" thought he, "so they must be in bed and
asleep." Stealing to the arbour, he began
carefully to build up beside it a small stack
of tarred sticks and shavings, just where the
rising wind would fan the flame, when the
loud crowing of a cock close by made him
start and listen ; but all was silent again, and
he went on with his work. When it was done
to his satisfaction, he struck a match ; guard-
ing it with trembling hands from the breeze
which threatened. to put it out, and stoop-
ing slowly, he applied the light to the little
heap. Then, only waiting an instant to
make sure that the shavings had caught
fire, he fled away from the spot as though he
were pursued, and never once looked behind
him until he reached the village. Creeping

F

quietly in by a back way, he managed to elude observation, and watching his opportunity got up to his room, and lay down on his bed as he had done many a night before, unnoticed by any of the household,—a prayerless, ungodly, miserable boy. He could not sleep. Every sound startled him, and he wondered as he lay in the dark whether Philip had been awakened by the red glare of the burning summer-house, or by the crackling of the flames. The possibility had escaped him before, but now it seemed unlikely that they could sleep through it. Restless and feverish with excitement, he tossed about, from one side to the other ; then it struck him that the match might have been blown out by a puff of wind, before it had time thoroughly to kindle the shavings. There was relief in the thought, and as he flung off the light bed-clothes to cool his fevered limbs, he exclaimed, "I hope it isn't burning ! I shall be glad after all, though I did want to serve him out." But the little pile of sticks ? that would lead to suspicion ! and _he_ would be suspected, too, as his feelings toward Quin were well known. "Oh," he cried, "I wish I hadn't done it— what a fool I have been!" His teeth began to chatter, and he pulled the bed-clothes up again—"Well, I must go the first thing in the morning before it's light," thought he, "and take 'em away if they haven't caught; and if I do meet anyone about, I'll tell 'em I'm looking for a robin's nest or something. How the wind is rising, too! what if it is burning after all ?"

But hark! the boy sprang up, for the loud clang of the fire-bell broke upon his ear. His heart died within him—it was discovered! All Fairfield was speedily aroused! "Fire! fire!" shouted a voice in the street, and Tom heard his father open his window, and ask in what direction it was.

"Can't quite make out," said the man; "down by the river somewhere. Mayhap it's only a barn; but I'm off to see." Then came the loud rattle of the engine, as the firemen dragged it down the village street; and Tom's door opened and his father called out, "Come on, Tom; I'm going to see the fun; they say it's the widow Quin's cottage that's alight!" Tom pretended to wake from a deep sleep. "What's the matter?" said he, as well as his choking voice would let him.

"Why, it's a fire, lad, a fire. You can't be sleeping through all this din, surely? Come along with me, I'm going down."

"I don't care to see it," said Tom, gruffly, "I'm sleepy;" and he turned over again as if in a heavy slumber. Mr. Hardy hurried off.

The cottage on fire! Oh no, it could not be; it was too terrible to be true! Surely the cottage was too far off to be in any danger? Tom shivered from head to foot, and the perspiration streamed down his face. He never dreamed that it would come to this; and if it should be discovered that he had lit that dreadful fire, what then? He would be thrown into prison, and brought to trial before a judge. Mingled with his terror of an earthly tribunal came a vague recollection of words from God's book, of awful woe to those who "devoured widows' houses." Eagerly he listened, straining his ear to catch every distant sound, till he could bear the suspense no longer, and, hurrying on his clothes, he rushed out into the street. He knew only too well, the direction in which to go; and when he reached the bridge, he could see the lurid sky, and the fierce flames leaping up through the thick smoke, though the cottage was partly hidden by trees. It was too true, and he covered his face with his hands to shut out the terrible sight. "Oh," he exclaimed, "I did not mean to do anything so dreadful as this; I never thought the fire would go further than the bower; what shall I do? what shall I do?" But it was useless to loiter, and he rushed madly on. Once his foot caught in a stump, and he fell heavily, but he was up in a moment, and ran on again until he reached the spot.

What a sight it was! The engine was working, but not effectively, for part of the machinery needed repair ; and the red flames shot up, hissing and roaring, licking up the water with their forked tongues, and destroying all before them. Not a hope remained of saving any part of the building. Tom saw Philip, with Harry Lynton and several other lads, but he avoided them, and asked a fireman where Mrs. Quin was.

"They've taken her up to Lyntonville ; it's a terrible business for her, poor thing ! " said the man, as he hurried away.

The parlour as yet had not suffered much, for the back of the house had caught fire first; and it came into Tom's mind to try and rescue something. He forced his way into the room through the scorching heat and smoke. Most of the furniture had been removed, but a few things still remained, and lying on a chair was Philip's beautiful Bible and his prize. Could it really be so short a time since the books were placed in his hands, and became the innocent cause of all this evil? Oh! that Tom could have recalled those hours : he would not have acted as he

had done. But there was no time to think.
He caught up the books, which had fortunately
received little injury, and as he tried to pass
out his foot struck against something on the
floor. It was a small miniature portrait.
He picked it up and made his way to the door;
but the flames had burst into the passage
and drove him back, while a shout was raised
outside that the roof was falling. Not a
moment was to be lost, and he dashed through
the smoke and flame only just in time to
escape being crushed beneath the falling
rafters; as it was his hair and clothes were
singed, and he was considerably burnt. After
this the fire began to subside, and Tom stood
gazing at the scene, with Philip's books in
his hand, like one bewildered. Philip, too,
stood there with folded arms, looking with a
sad, sad face, at the ruins of his home—
his mother's little all consumed in an hour!
Harry was trying to comfort him, but
Philip could not be comforted. Presently
Hardy came up, with blackened face, and his
hand tied up in his handkerchief: "Look
here, Quin, I found these," said he, as he put
the books and the miniature into his hands.

"My books!" cried Philip, "and papa's
likeness! Oh, Hardy, how did you get them?
My mother will be so pleased to have this

again. How can I thank you?" And his conscience smote him as he remembered his sinful feelings on the previous day.

"Why, Hardy," said Harry, "you're hurt. Did you get burnt? What's the matter?"

The boy looked very white, and turned away, muttering, "It's nothing—never mind: I'm glad I got them." But Philip followed him.

"Let me see your hand, Hardy, I'm sure it hurts you very much. I am so sorry!" Hardy winced as he tried to unbind his hand, which was severely burnt. He felt happier, in spite of the pain, than he had done, but he could not stand Philip's thanks.

"I say, Quin, leave it alone," said he, "I'll see to it when I get home."

"But you don't know what to do," cried Harry; "come along with us and I'll get my mother to bind it up for you. She knows all about burns."

"No, no," said Hardy, "there's my father; I'll go home with him."

"Hollo! youngster," said Mr. Hardy, when he saw his son, "so you came after all? I thought you wouldn't be long after me. But what's this you've been after—getting yourself burnt, eh? Why, what a fool you must have been to get into the thick of it that way! But never mind, never mind, lad," added he, rubbing his hands, as he thought of the custom the fire would be likely to bring to his store, "it's an ill wind that blaws naebody good." So saying, Mr. Hardy and Tom went on their way.

CHAPTER VII.

PHILIP'S DISCOVERY.

"Hush! idle thoughts, and words of ill,
Your Lord is listening; peace, be still."
"Be sure your sin will find you out."

As soon as it was light next morning, Philip, who could not sleep after the excitement and fatigue he had undergone, went down to reconnoitre the scene of the fire. Nothing remained of his little home but blackened and still smoking embers. It was a sad sight, for Philip knew that with the house his mother had lost her all. It had always been his comfort hitherto, that at least her home was her own; and he had looked forward to the happy day when, by his own exertions, he might be able in some measure to repay her tender care and love for him. Now all his bright hopes were dashed to the ground—and in how short a time! He felt very sorrowful as he looked at the ruins, and at the spot where the arbour had been. He thought of the many happy hours he had

spent there : would he ever be happy again ?
—for it seemed as though this terrible fire
had destroyed all his prospects for life. His
great ambition had been to study hard, and
by means of his education to make his way in
the world. But now, if he continued at
school, his mother would be obliged to work.
The thought was not to be endured for a
moment! No! he must put his shoulder to
the wheel, and at once ! There was only one
thing open to him : he must become a clerk
in a store—a shop-boy, as it would be called
in England. All his pride rose up against
such an idea ; " they were poor, but he was
still a gentleman," and a sharp conflict
ensued between his rebellious spirit and his
strong sense of duty. While his mind was
thus occupied, his eye caught the glitter of
something lying on the ground. Mechanically
he stooped and picked it up ; it was an open
knife, with " T. HARDY " roughly cut upon
the handle. He slipped it into his pocket,
intending to give it back when they next
met, and the incident hardly interrupted his
train of thought.

"Why, Philip, my boy," said Mr. Lynton,
who had come up to him unawares, " I did
not expect to find you here ! I thought you
were safe in bed ; and that's where you should

be," he added kindly, looking at his pale, wan face, "this sad business has been too much for you."

"I couldn't sleep, sir, and I thought I would come down and look at the old place again before anyone was about."

"That's my reason for coming also, my boy, for we may find some clue to account for it. It's a strange business, very strange," said Mr. Lynton, musing: "Was the house on fire when you were first roused?"

"Yes: I woke up quite suddenly, and found the room full of smoke. I had only just time to rush into my mother's room and arouse her, and to wake Biddy, before the flames burst in through the roof. You know it was at the back of the house, sir; and by the time we got down the engine was close by. They had seen it at the village before we knew anything about it."

"And was that place, your arbour down there,"—and Mr. Lynton pointed in the direction it had been, "was it burning then, or did it catch fire afterwards?"

"Oh no, sir, it was nearly burnt down before I woke at all."

"Then the fire must have originated there! Have you been in the habit of keeping matches or anything combustible down there, lately, Philip ? "

" No, sir, I am sure I never did."

" And you did not carry a lighted candle there last night ? Harry tells me you went to fetch a book you had left there."

" No, sir, I found the book lying on the bench. The moon was so bright I did not need the lantern."

Mr. Lynton was silent for some minutes. " It's my impression," said he, at length, " from all I can gather, that it must have been the work of an incendiary. It is a sad loss to your poor mother, Philip."

Philip's lip quivered. " That's just what I've been thinking about, sir. I'm afraid I must leave off going to school now, and see if I can't find some place in a store."

" Ah ! " said Mr. Lynton ; " and were these the thoughts that made you look so sad when I first met you ? "

" I daresay they did, sir. I am very sorry. I did so wish to work hard, and get on in my lessons, and enter some profession fit for a gentleman ; and now I shall be nothing better than a tradesman all my life." And Philip's voice trembled, and the unbidden tears would start into his eyes.

Mr. Lynton looked at him in some surprise,

for the boy had never before spoken so openly, and putting his hand kindly upon his shoulder, he said : "I see this fire is likely to be the cause of even a greater trial to you than I at first anticipated, Philip; but cheer up, my boy! you know God helps those who try to help themselves. Besides, you must not think that because you enter a store, it must necessarily make you any the less a gentleman. I can quite sympathize with your feelings, for you have not been long enough in the country to understand our modes of thought; but I can assure you that in a colony like this, some of our most highly educated and esteemed men have begun life in a position such as you contemplate. But you have not had time yet to think over your plans; and in the meantime, Philip, you know we are only too glad to have your mother and you at Lyntonville. And remember, my boy, you will never want a friend while it is in my power to help you."

"I thank you, sir, you are very kind; indeed, I don't know how to thank you enough," said Philip, as they reached the house.

Harry did all in his power to cheer his friend. "Do you know, Philip," said he, later in the day, when they were talking it all

over, "I've been thinking this morning about
that text, 'Not a sparrow shall fall to the
ground without your Father in heaven.' If
God looks after the sparrows he must know
all about this—how it happened and all—
and don't you think he'll take care of you?"

"Oh, yes," said Philip, "that's what
mamma says, and I don't know what we
should do if we did not believe God's promises;
but it's very hard to feel right about it, and
to think that it's all for the best. Perhaps
some day we shall know why it happened
better than we can now."

Towards evening Philip slipped away
quietly, to take another look at the ruins.
Again and again he went over all the circumstances of the fire in his own mind;
when suddenly he remembered Hardy's knife,
and he took it out of his pocket. He knew
it well, for he had seen it many a time before,
but now it acquired a new interest in his
sight. How came it in the spot where he
had found it in the morning? The crowd
was collected in front of the cottage, and on
the bank of the river—what could Hardy
have been about there? It was open, too,
when he picked it up, as if it had just been
used; and Philip examined the knife, as
though the inanimate steel could give him

some clue to the truth. His thoughts re-
curred to Mr. Lynton's idea, that the place
had been set on fire purposely. Then the
events of the day before flashed across his
mind; the examination; the prizes he had
so unexpectedly won, which Hardy had looked
upon as his own; the angry scowl, too, upon
his face, as he met him coming from the
school-house; above all, the difficulty in
accounting for the fire. It could not have
been accidental; some one must have done
it; and that some one? Philip was fast
working himself into a state of painful excitement. Was it possible? Yes, it was, it
must have been Hardy! He began to see it
all now; this was the cruel, cowardly revenge
he had planned, and as Philip became more
and more convinced of the truth of his sus-
picions, his angry passions rose in proportion.
"How wicked of him!" he thought; "I never
injured him, that he should do such a cruel,
cowardly thing. I've borne all his taunts;
I never said an unkind word to him in my
life; and this is what comes of it all!" His
brain seemed on fire, as one argument after
another to prove Hardy's guilt arose in his
mind; and his eye gleamed with a strange
light while he pondered over the facts which
were so suspicious. "But this is more than

I can bear. I'll show him up in his true
ght; mean, cowardly bully that he is! If
ere only myself it would be different, but
he h... ruined my mother, and I hate him!
I do!" said he, aloud, stamping with his foot
upon the ground, "and I shouldn't care if he
were hung for it!" The sound of his own
voice startled him.

And was this Philip, the meek disciple of
a meek and lowly Master? It was indeed;
and for awhile it seemed as though Satan had
triumphed. All his evil passions were in
league against him; anger, hatred, revenge,
all struggled for the mastery, under the
guise of righteous indignation, and a just
desire to avenge his mother's wrongs. But
God, in his mercy, will not let his children
be tempted above that they are able to bear;
and so it was with Philip. He had received
great provocation. His mother, his loved
mother, had been injured almost beyond
repair, and his own prospects in life blighted
—and for what? Simply to gratify the bad
passions of a boy whom he had never wronged.
It was a severe trial, and we must not think
the worse of him because the old self which
remained in his heart fought a hard battle
with the new self implanted by God's grace,
and nearly gained the victory, but in the hour

of his weakness he received strength from
above to resist the strong temptation. The
sound of his own voice brought him to himself, and above the angry tumult within his
breast he seemed to hear a still, sr .11 voice,
whispering, " But I say unto you. Lo. your
enemies ; do good to them that hate you, and
pray for them that despitefully us you and
persecute you." Hitherto 1 had been
walking rapidly on, not caring where he went;
now he stopped, and sitting down on an old
stump by the side of the path, he took out a
little pocket Testament, and turned to the
words. The gleam faded from his eye, and
the angry look from his face, as the holy
words carried conviction to his conscience.
"Oh ! " he said, " how wicked I have been !
I have blamed him for the very thing I was
going to do myself. May God forgive me !"
A tear stole down his cheek, a tear of
repentance for his sin, and he knelt down in
the shade of the forest trees to pray for pardon, and wisdom to direct. It was no easy
decision he had to make. Ought he to con-
ceal what he suspected, or was it his duty to
make it known ? Very earnestly he besought
his Heavenly Father to guide him in the
right way, and he turned over the pages of his
little Testament to see if he could find any

message from God's word to help him in his difficulty. Presently his eye rested on this verse in one of his favourite chapters: "Dearly beloved, avenge not yourselves, but rather give place unto wrath; for it is written, Vengeance is mine; I will repay, saith the Lord. Therefore if thine enemy hunger, feed him; if he thirst, give him drink; for in so doing thou shalt heap coals of fire on his head" (Rom. xii. 19, 20). He thought awhile, and then he decided to keep what he knew to himself. "I will never mention it: God helping me, I will keep it a secret all my life." A hollow place in a tree close at hand caught his eye. "I will put the knife in there, and if it should ever be found no one will know how it came there." He had to climb up to reach it, and the knife dropped down into the cavity. Then he turned to go home, and as he went he remembered Hardy's pale, frightened face, and how he had injured himself in saving the books. "He never could have meant to set the cottage on fire," thought Philip; "most likely the sparks were blown upon the shingles, for the wind set that way, and then the roof caught. I daresay he was afraid of being found out, and he must have been sorry, too, or he would not have risked getting burnt to save anything.

Poor fellow! I'll go and ask how his hand is by-and-by. Shall I tell him I suspect him? No, I think not; it will be kinder never to let him know. Oh Lord, help me to keep my resolution!" he inwardly prayed, "and enable me to serve Thee aright, now and always." In this softened frame, Philip returned to Lyntonville. It was as though a terrible storm had passed over his soul—the wind and the waves boisterous and contrary, and tossing the frail bark of his spiritual life to and fro, in their angry tumult; but the Saviour's voice had spoken above the tempest, saying, "Peace, be still;" and immediately there was a calm. Oh! well is it for us all if we have taken that gentle Saviour as our Guide and Helper, that we may be enabled "so to pass the waves of this troublesome world, that finally we may come to the land of everlasting life," in the world to come.

CHAPTER VIII.

"Conscience does make cowards of us all."

WE must now return to Hardy, whom we last saw going home with his father after the fire. As soon as he reached the house, his hand was properly bound up; his father at the same time rating him soundly for what he called his stupidity in getting burnt.

"Take care of number one; that's my maxim, lad, and you'll find it a safe one, I can tell you. But now you'd better turn in, for I should say you'd had enough of it for one night. Stay, you're cold. Come into the store, and I'll give you something to set you all to rights;" and he poured out some whisky, and made Tom drink it. It was not the first time the boy had taken spirits, but in his present excited state, it affected him greatly. He went up and threw himself on his bed, and immediately fell into a heavy sleep. It was still early when he woke; and he roused himself with a dull sense of something on his mind, but what, he could not remember for some minutes. Slowly it all came back to his memory, and the pain of his burnt hand was only too sure a reminder of the part he had played in the scenes of the night. He got up and looked at himself in the little glass which hung against the wall. He thought his very face would betray him, he looked so pale and haggard; but people would imagine it was the pain of the burn; they could never suspect him of having any share in it, unless—and the mere possibility was terrible to him—unless he had been observed going in that direction so shortly before the alarm! He went down-stairs and wandered into the kitchen, where the boy was lighting the stove before opening the shutters in the store. He tried to whistle unconcernedly as Jack made some common remark about the fire, and went into the shop.

The early morning sunlight streamed in through the round holes in the shutters, which he attempted to take down in the caprice of the moment, and leaving them half-opened, went off to the wood-shed. Here he began to cut through a log of wood which had been left upon the saw-horse; and then he felt in his pocket for his knife. It was

gone! He rushed up to his room and
sought for it in every hole and corner—it
was not there! And then he remembered
having cut the string which bound the little
bundle of tarred sticks with it the night
before. He must have left it in his hurry
close to the spot, and his name cut in large
letters on the handle would be a witness
against him! "Fool that I have been!" he
muttered; "if I had only thought what it
would come to, I would have seen myself far
enough before I stirred one step to do it.
But there's no one about so early as this; I
may find it yet;" and he ran off full speed
to look for the missing knife. He paused at
the ditch where he had fallen in his blind
haste before, and searched all about, but no
knife was there; and he walked on as fast as
he could to the place where the cottage had
been.

Mr. Lynton and Philip had not left the
spot many minutes when Hardy came up,
and he saw their retreating figures crossing
the bridge. Carefully he looked about in
every direction; but, as our readers are
already aware, without a chance of success,
for it was at that moment safe in Philip's
pocket! After a long and fruitless search,
he gave it up as hopelessly lost. One com-

fort was it was nowhere near the arbour, so
that even if found it would not rouse suspicion, and his heart was lightened of half
its load. His chief anxiety was lest he should
be found out, yet as he stood looking at the
smouldering ruins, his conscience smote him
sorely. " I wish I'd never thought of doing
it; such a pretty little place, too! I never
dreamed the fire would spread like that; and
I don't believe anything was saved." No,
Tom Hardy, it is easier to do wrong than to
set it right after it is done; and that you have
found to your cost. " Well," he thought, at
last, "I can't help it now, and I shan't care
much if I can only keep it quiet." Poor boy!
he forgot that there was One above who
knew all, and from whom no secrets are hid.
He had never been taught in his childhood
of the " Eye that never sleeps," resting
always and ever upon each one of us, and
now all he cared for was to escape the anger
of his fellow creatures, and the just punishment of his fault.

As he reached his father's door, he over-
heard several men talking about the fire, and
stopped to listen.

" I say, Smith, were you up at the fire last
night?" said one.

" Not I; I heard nothing of it till this

morning. They do say as how it must ha' been a 'cendiary, and if so be it is, they 'll put out a reward for certain."

"You don't say so?" said the other; "well I was thinking myself it were mighty strange how it come'd about."

"Biddy, that's Mrs. Quin's sarvant, towld me the morn, that sorra a bit of a fire had been in the stove fornent tin o'clock o' the mornin' yesterday, for the misthress had been up to Lyntonville all the day, and she was fain to be widout it, for the hate," said an Irish lad, who was errand-boy and news-monger in general to the village.

"Aye, then, I shouldn't wonder if there might be some truth in it. I guess Mr. Lynton won't let him off very easy, whoever he is."

"Aisy is it?" said Terence; "shure I'd flay him alive, if he was the praste himself, for layin' a finger on the lot of the widow and the orphan—bad luck to him, whoever he was—who never did harm to nobody!"

Tom Hardy shook from head to foot. Then it was suspected! And if his knife were to be found after all about the place, it would bring conviction home to him, and then what would become of him? All day long the boy was tormented by these fears, and every fresh comment upon the fire only added to his misery. His time hung heavily on his hands, for the school was closed, and he hardly dared to join any of his companions lest some tell-tale look or unguarded word might betray him. But the days wore on; no clue had been found, and he began to be more easy in his mind. Little did he imagine that one person suspected his share in the transaction, and that person the very one he had so deeply injured.

Philip took the first opportunity of inquiring for Hardy's hand, and of thanking him once more for having rescued the books. He did it sincerely and warmly, feeling that he had now quite forgiven him from his heart for the mischief he had caused; Hardy had only meant to injure him, and for this Philip no longer harboured any angry feelings —the rest had been in God's hands. Those few kind words from Philip went straight to Hardy's conscience, and he winced under them as though each had been a lash.

"Do you know, Hardy, I am afraid I shan't be able to come to school any more?"

"Not come back to school! why not?" said he, in astonishment.

"Why, I must try and do something to help my mother now. I wouldn't have said

H

anything about it, only I heard that your
father wanted a clerk, and, perhaps, he might
take me." Mr. Hardy had the largest and
most important store in the place, and there
was no other where Philip could find employment.

"Take you into the store, Quin! do you
really mean it? I thought you were too
proud, a long way, to do anything of the
kind!" Hardy did not now speak bitterly,
but in unfeigned surprise.

"Yes," said Philip, "I have been very
foolish, I know, but one grows wiser as one
grows older and I don't know what else I
can do. Do you think your father would
have me?"

"I don't know," said Hardy, "he wants a
man."

"Perhaps Mr. Lynton would speak for
me," said Philip, thoughtfully; "I think I'll
ask him;" and soon after the boys parted.

So Philip wished to come into the store!
Hardy was far from echoing the wish; he
did not want to have a constant reminder of
his folly before his eyes, but he said nothing;
and next day Mr. Lynton and Philip made
their appearance.

"I believe, Hardy, you are in want of a
clerk? Perhaps you would be good enough

A PLACE IN THE STORE.

to try my young friend here, and see whether
you can make anything of him as a man of
business."

Philip felt his cheeks burning; it was a
hard trial for him, and one from which Mr.
Lynton would willingly have shielded him,
could he have found anything more suitable
at the time.

Mr. Hardy rubbed his hands, and scanned
Philip with his cold harsh eyes. " He's very
young, sir, very young. I guess he won't
be worth his salt for a long time to come.
Can you write a goodish hand, youngster ; let
us see ? " and he pushed the ink towards
him. Philip's hand shook so that he could
hardly hold the pen, but he managed to write
a few words in a bold hand.

"Ah ! come, that's pretty well for a
beginning," said he. "It's Mrs. Quin's son,
I believe, is it not? a sad thing that fire,
very. And you want to do something for
yourself, eh ? Well, sir, under the circumstances, and since it's to oblige you, I'll
consent to try him ; but he's young, sir, far
too young. However, I'm glad to do a chari-
table action at all times ! " Philip's blood
boiled. Did the man think he was doing him
a charity, when a word from him would ruin
his son for life ? Hasty words were rushing

to his lips, when he suddenly checked himself, and inwardly prayed for strength to be
enabled to keep his resolution.

Poor Philip! it was no easy task he had
in prospect, but he thought of the promise,
"As thy days, so shall thy strength be," and
he was helped. It was settled that the next
Monday should see him take his place behind
the counter for the first time, at a salary of
four dollars a week; and with a heavy heart
he walked back to Lyntonville.

"It will be a trial to you, Philip," said
Mr. Lynton, "especially at first, but strive
to do your duty in your new position, and you
will find that God will bless you in it. The
discipline may seem hard just now, but
believe me, in after life you will never regret
it, and just let me give you one word of
advice: don't add to your mother's sorrow
by letting her see what a sacrifice you are
making for her sake. No doubt she feels it
enough already."

Philip remembered Mr. Lynton's caution,
and when he told his mother of the arrange-
ment that had been made, he did it as cheer-
fully as he could.

"It will be pleasant to feel that I am
beginning to help you, dear mother."

"Well, my son," she replied, stroking back

the hair from his forehead with her gentle, caressing hand, " it is not what I could have wished for you, but our heavenly Father knows best, we may be perfectly satisfied of that ; and He is able to bring good out of what seems to us only evil."

CHAPTER IX.

MR. HARDY'S STORE.

"Teach me, my God and King,
  In all things Thee to see;
And what I do in anything,
  To do it as for Thee.

All may of Thee partake;
  No thing can be so mean
That with this tincture, for Thy sake,
  Will not grow bright and clean."

MONDAY came, and Philip went to his post. He felt strangely awkward, as he was told to assist in unpacking and marking a large case of new goods just arrived from Toronto. Hardy employed two clerks, and Bennett, whose place Philip was to take, still remained for a few days to put his successor into the ways of the business. Joe Gammon, the other, was a youth about eighteen years of age—good-looking and sharp, and unscrupulous enough in his dealings to please his like-minded master. "Joe's a lad of the right sort," Hardy used to say; "no fear but he'll make his way in the world."

Bennett was an older man, and would have been a far safer companion for Philip than Joe, but he had saved money, and was now about to better himself by taking a share in a small country business in a rising village a few miles off.

"You've got hold of a raw hand there, Bennett," said Joe, laughing. "Never left his mother's apron-string before, pretty dear!"

"You'll teach him a thing or two before you've done with him, I expect, Master Joe," replied Bennett. "I tell you what, youngster," added he, in a low tone, to Philip, as Joe walked off to the other end of the store to attend to a customer, "you'd better look to yourself here. I'm no saint myself, but of all the precious young scamps I ever came across, that chap's the worst."

There was a rough kindliness of manner about Bennett for which Philip felt grateful, and he was really sorry when he left the place, at the end of the week. During that time, he had set to work with a will to learn as much as he could of his new duties, and by degrees he became more expert, and lost his awkward ways. It was still early in the summer, and Philip used to sigh sometimes as he thought of the green shady woods, and

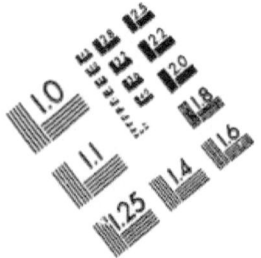

**IMAGE EVALUATION
TEST TARGET (MT-3)**

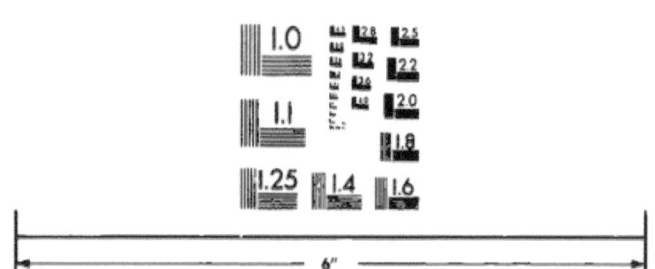

6"

Photographic
Sciences
Corporation

22 WEST MAIN STREET
WEBSTER, N.Y. 14580
(716) 872-4503

the cool splash of the river by their little
cottage. It was hot and close in the store,
and the mingled odours of soap and cheese,
and candles and butter, were often so over-
powering, that he was obliged to go to the
door for a breath of the pure fresh air, while
he leant his aching head against the side-
post. His work was very hard, and its
irksomeness made it still more so; but he
uttered no complaint, and even Mr. Hardy's
sharp eyes could detect but few faults. But
he had greater trials than these. What he
felt most was being obliged to work for and
with such unprincipled men, as gradually he
found out Mr. Hardy and Joe to be. At
first he suspected nothing, for he was so
conscientious himself that it never once
entered his head that they could wilfully
deceive and cheat; but little by little his
eyes were opened, and his whole soul re-
volted from such wrong dealings. Very soon
Hardy's customers began to like Philip to
serve them, for they found that he gave good
measure, and would recommend none but the
best articles, whilst he was always obliging
and courteous.

One day an old woman drove up to the
door in one of the country wagons, and
alighting, popped her head into the shop.

Philip was busy measuring off some print for another customer. Seeing him engaged she went off, though Joe was standing idle; but after a while returned again to find Philip still occupied. This time she came in, but nothing would induce her to mention her wants until she could secure Philip's services.

"What can I show you, to-day, Mrs. McGregor?" said Joe, all smiles.

"It's a fine day for the mowing," replied she; "I thought we should ha' had rain last night."

"So did I," said Joe. "Is it groceries you want, to-day? we have a prime lot of goods on hand just now, which we are selling cheap."

"What's that stuff-piece you have over there?" said the old lady, keeping one eye on Philip.

"Ah! the blue on a green ground. Sweet thing!" said Joe, taking it down. "We have just received it, with a large assortment of goods, by the last steamer from the old country" (it had been in the store a year and a half); "ten yards to a dress. It will suit you exactly, Mrs. McGregor; let me cut off a dress-length for you. Come, I'll let you have it for six dollars; and that's less than cost price."

"No," said she, feeling the texture, "I don't think I'll take it to-day;" and looking about for something else to remark upon, she espied a little machine at the other end of the counter.

"And what may this be, Mr. Joe?"

"Well, ma'am," said Joe, "that is the most extraordinary little article that's been invented this long time; but won't you allow me to measure you off this piece? You can't do better, I assure you." Then seeing Mrs. McGregor's attention wholly diverted— "It's an apple-parer, ma'am, and will do the work of six pair of hands in no time at all; and all for the small sum of a quarter dollar."

"Law! you don't say so," said she, with pretended interest, "you couldn't show me how it works, now, could you?"

"Oh, certainly, ma'am, with the greatest pleasure," and he went to get an apple for the purpose. The paring process was only half over, when Mrs. McGregor, to her great relief, saw Philip opening the door for the other customer, who had completed her purchases, and suddenly leaving Joe and his machine, she walked across to the opposite counter, saying to Philip, "I'll tell *you* what I want, Mr. Quin, for I believe you won't cheat me; but as to that young chap yonder, he shall play off none of his tricks upon me." Joe did not like to be outshone thus by the new-comer, and found ways and means of venting his spite upon Philip, who, on the whole, led no easy life.

Mrs. Quin had taken lodgings in the village in order to be near her son, and Philip went home to her every evening after the store was closed. But the close confinement soon began to tell upon his delicate frame, and he often longed to be at his beloved books, when he was occupied all day long in weighing out pounds of sugar, and measuring yards of factory cottons for the poor settlers of the district. His mother watched his pale face grow thinner, and his step less light every day, with sad forebodings. She would have given all she had to be able to take him away from his distasteful occupation, but his weekly earnings contributed material¹ to their support, and what could they do without them? No repining word ever passed his lips, and even his fond mother never guessed how much he suffered.

In the meantime, things went on much as usual at the Long Cross School; though Hardy now found a new and scarcely less formidable rival in Harry Lynton. In one

I

thing, however, Tom was changed, for he never went into the store if he could help it, and avoided Philip as much as possible; but all sorrowful recollections of the injury his conduct had caused seemed to have faded from his memory.

Harry never ceased to miss his friend. "I declare," said he, one day, "I never see you now, Phil; but I suppose it can't be helped. I don't know how I get on without you, though, for you always contrived to keep me straight."

"You can't be more sorry than I am, Harry," replied Philip, sadly, "it seems as if all my happy days were over. Only I believe it's my duty, and that makes me more reconciled to it." Scarcely a day passed without Harry making some little errand to the store, that he might have an opportunity of chatting with Philip, and these short visits, and the evening hour with his mother, were the only pleasures he had to relieve the monotonous labour of his life. And so week after week passed on, but Philip remembered he was helping his mother, and this was his greatest comfort. He scarcely knew himself how weak and ill he was, and toiled on, thankful for the employment which helped to keep the wolf

from the door. Very often they had to deny
themselves necessaries, and it would have
melted the hardest heart to have been
an unseen witness of their daily meal.
"Mother," Philip would say sometimes,
"I'm not hungry to-day, I can't eat any
dinner;" and all Mrs. Quin's persuasions
would only induce him to taste the scanty
fare. Again, if he happened to be later
than usual, she would keep the lion's share
for her boy, while perhaps little food had
passed her own lips that day. None knew
how hard a battle they had to fight with
poverty; and Philip tried his utmost to earn
a higher salary. Mr. Hardy knew full well
he was worth it; but whilst he could secure
his services for four dollars a week, why
should he think of raising it? And the poor
boy, in his inexperience, trusting to his
master's honour, toiled harder than ever to
win his approbation.

September was now drawing towards its
close, and the bright autumn tints told a tale
of coming winter, when Mr. Lynton having
made arrangements for his usual hunting
expedition, determined this year to take
Harry with him, so pleased was he with his
industry and the progress he had made at
school. Harry, nearly wild with delight,

rushed into the store as soon as he possibly could, to tell Philip the good news. Poor Philip's face fell.

"Going away for a month! Oh, Harry, what shall I do without seeing you sometimes? I shall miss you so much!"

"Never mind, old fellow," said Harry, "a month will soon pass, and then I shall be able to tell you all about it, you know. But I say, isn't it jolly though?" Philip did not look as if he thought it very jolly, but he tried to sympathize in his friend's pleasure. "There goes the bell; I came in early on purpose to tell you, Phil, but I must be off now."

In the course of the day it chanced that Tom was sent into the store by his father, as an extra hand was required, and for the first time for several weeks he noticed Philip, who was looking more than usually pale and weak. "Why, Quin," said he, "how bad you look! what's the matter?"

"I don't know," replied he, "I'm all right, thank you."

"But you don't look all right, I can tell you. Why don't you take something? I believe you ought to have port wine, you haven't got a bit of colour in your face. Why don't you?"

Philip smiled a melancholy smile as he thought of their narrow means. "We can't afford it," he said quietly. Hardy turned away quickly and asked no more questions. "I believe he's going to die," thought he; "this hard work is killing him—he's not used to it." More slowly the idea forced itself into his mind that this was hi' handi-work, and once there he could not get rid of it; it followed him wherever he went, and once he woke with a start in the night dreaming that he was being dragged off to prison, accused of Philip's murder!

Harry had been gone very nearly a month, and Philip rejoiced much at the prospect of welcoming him back again so soon. October was passing quickly away, the trees were already leafless and bare, and sharp frosts had set in, which made poor Philip shiver and cough. He himself began to think that he should not be able to go on much longer, for sometimes he became so giddy he was obliged to sit down by the road-side, cold as it was, on his way to the store in the morning; and he felt he could not lift the same heavy weights he did formerly. One day when he went as usual to the post-office for the letters he found one addressed to himself, and greatly to his surprise on open-

I 2

ing it, he saw that it contained nothing but a ten-dollar note! His heart was full of wonder and thankfulness as he thought of the many little comforts this sum would procure for his mother, and all day he tried to think who the kind donor could be. His mother had not seen him look so joyful for weeks as when he threw the letter into her lap and made her guess what was in it.

"But who can have sent this money to us, Philip? I am afraid to use it without knowing."

"Why, mother, surely some one who wishes to be kind to us. O, do spend it!" he cried, looking quite disappointed. "It must be meant for us, for see,—it is directed to me quite plainly."

Mrs. Quin looked troubled as she examined the envelope. "I think, my boy," she said at length, "we had better not touch this note at present unless we are driven to it. My heart misgives me, lest there should be anything wrong."

Philip's bright look had quite vanished now, but he never questioned for a moment his mother's wishes. "Well, mother, I suppose you know best," he said, "but I am very sorry."

Mrs. Quin locked up the letter, just as it

was, in her desk, and they tried to think no more about it, though that was no easy task when they needed help so much.

A few evenings after this occurrence, Philip came home so ill that Mrs. Quin felt sadly grieved. "My dear boy," she said, as he sat down at her feet and leant against her knee, "you must not go again! See, I have been able to get some employment, too," and she showed him some needlework she had been busy wi h when he came in. "Phœbe Harris i— ng to be married, and she asked me if I — any one who could help her for the next few weeks, and I gladly offered. You know I am a famous needlewoman!"

Philip looked up in mute dismay. "Oh, mother, mother, that it should come to this! You must not do it. Indeed, indeed, it will kill me to see you working like a common sempstress! I cannot bear it." And in his weakness and excitement he laid down his head and sobbed.

"My darling," she said, soothing his distress by her gentle tones, "you must not give way like this. Rather let us thank God that he has put this offer of work in my way. Indeed, I have been full of thankfulness ever since, for I have tried before to find employment without success; and now Philip, I

must try and do it so well that I may make
a reputation," she added, playfully, though
her heart ached as she looked at her boy.

"Mother, God has dealt very hardly with
us."

"Hush, my Philip," she said solemnly,
"you must not say such words. 'The Lord
loveth whom he chasteneth.' Our trials
come from his loving hand, and you know,
dear, he can remove them quite as easily
when he sees fit." A long time they sat
thus, and talked together as only those who
are very near and dear to each other can;
and before going to rest, they knelt together
at the throne of grace to commit all their
cares and sorrows into the hands of him who
careth for his children.

Philip resolved to go back to the store on
the morrow, and to ask for a week's rest.
He did not know then how very soon his
connexion with Mr. Hardy would be ended.

CHAPTER X.

THE MISSING NOTE.

" Bear through sorrow, wrong, and ruth
In thy heart the dew of youth,
On thy lips the smile of truth."

THOUGH feeling very ill next morning, Philip managed to crawl down to the store, but he had hardly entered the door before Joe accosted him, his eyes gleaming with malicious delight,—

" Oh, I say, isn't there a jolly row, that's all ! Here's the ' boss' been storming away all the morning, and asking for you. I expect you'll catch it if ever you did in your life !" and Joe shrugged his shoulders and rolled his eyes in the most suggestive manner.

" Why, what's the matter ? " asked Philip, feeling rather uncomfortable, though not conscious of having done anything wrong.

" Ah ! that's just it ! who did it, I should like to know ?"

" Well, but Joe, do tell me what it is !"

"I like your innocence!" replied Joe,
"'do tell,' indeed! Just as if I should know
anything about it.   Only I guess you'll find
out fast enough as soon as the 'boss' has
done his breakfast ; you'd better ask him what
it is!"

Presently Mr. Hardy made his appearance.

"Oh! you've come, have you?" said he,
harshly, " just walk this way; I want to
speak to you," and he collared Philip, and
half led, half dragged him into the little
inner room.

"Look here, boy, I've missed some money
from the till, and ten-dollar notes can't walk
off by themselves. Now, do you know anything about it? You had better speak the
truth, mind, for I'm determined to sift this
matter to the bottom!"

Philip stood aghast. "I, sir? I never
took any money from the till! I assure you
I would not do such a thing! I know nothing
of a ten-dollar note. Indeed I don't think
I have seen a ten"—Philip suddenly stopped,
coloured and hesitated—the remembrance of
the note they had received through the post
flashed across his mind.

"Ha!" said Mr. Hardy, seizing him
roughly by the arm, "you do know something about it then, after all, you young

rascal, do you ? I thought as much. Come, speak out !"

" Oh, sir, have you—do you ever mark your notes ? "

" Mark them ? Oh ! you want to find out that, do you, to see whether it is worth while to confess ! You've taken a note with my private mark on it, and you'd like to know if you can keep it without being detected ! But I'll have the law of you, that I will, if I find this has been any of your doings ; and if it is marked, what then ? You don't leave this room till—"

" Mr. Lynton, sir," said Joe, opening the door at that moment, and Harry and his father entered. In an instant Hardy's manner changed, and he dropped Philip's arm, who uttered a cry of joy as he saw his friends.

" Oh, sir, oh, Mr. Lynton !" cried he, springing to his side, "God has sent you here, I am sure, for I am accused of stealing, and you know I would not do such a thing !"

Mr. Lynton looked from one to the other in astonishment.

" What's all this about, Mr. Hardy ? "

" Well, you see, sir," said Hardy in a fawning tone, rubbing his hands in his usual manner, " appearances are sadly against him, and I was naturally roused; it was only to be expected, sir. Here I find this morning, counting over my receipts from the till, that a ten-dollar note is missing; and when I make inquiries, this young fellow gets as red as a turkey-cock—is confused, and hesitates; and what am I to think? It's not the first little thing I've missed lately, either !"

"This is a very serious accusation, Mr. Hardy," said Mr. Lynton, with some severity. "I should like to hear Quin's story."

"Oh! certainly, sir, certainly. I'm willing, I'm sure, to give the lad every chance of clearing himself; but it looks suspicious, sir, very suspicious."

"We'll judge of that presently," said Mr. Lynton. "Hush! Harry, be silent, if you please. Well, Philip, what have you to say for yourself, my boy?" he added, kindly.

"Oh, sir, you don't believe I could be guilty of such a thing !—you know I couldn't. But I asked Mr. Hardy if it were marked, because—because we had one sent to us in a letter a few days ago, and I noticed a little round 'o' in the corner." ("Whew!" whistled Hardy, "a nice trumped-up story that is, you don't come over me like that, my boy." Philip took no notice of the interruption.)

"You can ask my mother, Mr. Lynton we've got the note now!"

"Well, if that doesn't beat all!" said Hardy; "now, sir, you see I was not far wrong!"

"I can't say I view the case in that light, Mr. Hardy; when do you say this letter came, Philip?"

"It was Monday or Tuesday, sir, I forget which," and the boy trembled so from excitement he could hardly stand.

Mr. Lynton thought a moment; "I shall go at once to Mrs. Quin, taking Philip with me, to ascertain the truth of this matter, for I wish to see it satisfactorily cleared up, and I beg you will follow, Mr. Hardy."

"Very well, sir, I will attend you most willingly."

Mr. Lynton's conveyance was in the village, and they drove immediately to Mrs. Quin's lodging. The widow's heart sank as she saw Philip returning at this unusual hour in company with Mr. Lynton, for she feared some new evil had happened to her boy, and she hastened out to meet them.

" We want you to settle a knotty point for us, my dear madam," said Mr. Lynton, after his first friendly salutation; " an unpleasant incident has occurred in Mr. Hardy's store;

K

some money is missing, and Philip has mentioned that a note has come into your possession in an unaccountable manner, which seems to give a clue to the lost one."

"How thankful I am," said Mrs. Quin, "I kept the note! Here it is, in the very envelope it came in!" and she unlocked her desk, and placed it in Mr. Lynton's hands. "Although I thought it not improbable that some kind friend might have wished to surprise us, I could not feel comfortable in making use of it without some further knowledge."

Mr. Lynton handed the note to Hardy, who instantly recognised it as his own.

"That's it, sure enough," said he, "for here's my private mark on it; and now the question is who the thief may be, and that to my mind is as clear as daylight."

"And pray what is your solution of the difficulty, Mr. Hardy, for in truth I cannot see my way through the business?"

"Why, it's just this, sir; the lad wants money—he takes the note—posts it to himself—brings it home to his mother. I'm sorry to say it, ma'am, for your sake, for I daresay you knew nothing about the matter, but your son's the thief, or I'm very much mistaken."

"Oh, mother, you don't believe I could

have done it! Tell me, oh tell me, *you* know me to be innocent! God knows I am; has he forsaken us altogether?" cried the poor lad, clasping his hands in an agony of despair. "Oh, Mr. Lynton, do, do believe me! I never saw the note until I took it out of the envelope; indeed, indeed I didn't! I assure you I am speaking nothing but the truth, I never told a lie in my life!"

"God have mercy upon us," said Mrs. Quin, as the hot tears rolled down her face, "we have never seen such trouble as this!" Harry stood by meanwhile, burning with indignation—"Why didn't his father turn the fellow out; how dared he say that Philip was a thief!" But his father was too judicious to act hastily in such a case, knowing that he would injure rather than benefit Philip's cause; besides, he felt that it must be thoroughly investigated, and though his belief in the innocence of the boy remained unshaken, yet he could not but acknowledge that appearances were against him.

"You say this note has been abstracted from your till, Mr. Hardy; pray has no one else besides Quin had access to it?"

"Well, I can't say but there has; there's Joe, and maybe Jack, if he had a mind to steal, might find some way to get at it; but the thing is, you see, sir, that here's the very identical note, and it isn't a very likely thing that either of them would steal out of charity ! "

" No," said Mr. Lynton, as an idea struck him, " but it is possible that this has been done to fasten suspicion upon an innocent person. I must examine the lads you speak of at once ; and, Philip, you may rest assured that your previous character will go far to clear you from this imputation in the sight of your friends, until it is proved beyond a doubt that you are guilty."

Philip had quite regained his composure; but the hot flush had faded from his face, leaving him so deadly pale that Mr. Lynton was shocked to see the change that had taken place in his appearance in a few short weeks.

" I cannot say more than I have said, Mr. Lynton, and my mother knows it is true. We have often wanted money, and when that letter came I thanked God that he had put it into the heart of some kind friend to send it. I little thought then it would be the means of such trouble to us ; and now I can only wait patiently till—" The door suddenly opened, and all eyes turned towards the new comer. Tom Hardy, for it was he, walked straight up to his father.

"Look here, father," said he; "stop all this, don't accuse Philip Quin of doing what you know it is not in him to do. I took the note!"

"You!" exclaimed all the party, in various tones of surprise; and Harry shouted, "Tom Hardy for ever!" not caring in his glee who was the guilty party, so long as Philip was cleared.

"You, you young scoundrel, you robbed your father's till!" cried Mr. Hardy, turning upon him furiously; "come along with me, and—"

"Stop, Mr. Hardy, we have a right to hear the story out; speak out, boy." Tom Hardy looked Mr. Lynton full in the face, sullen but resolute.

"I'll tell you why I took it, Mr. Lynton. I saw Quin getting thinner and thinner; I knew four dollars a week was barely enough to keep him from starving, and that my father ought to give him more, and I thought to help him. I suppose you'll say it was wicked. I pretty nearly always am wicked now!" he added, bitterly, "but I can't help it! If you knew all—"

"Can't help robbing your father, you good-for-nothing boy?" screamed Mr. Hardy. "I'll teach you to say you can't help it!" and he

K 2

made a rush at his son a. if he were going to administer summary punishment then and there. Philip, who had sunk down on a seat by his mother's side, half-bewildered by the sudden turn events had taken, started up. "Oh! Mr. Hardy, don't be angry with him, pray don't be angry; I'll do anything if you'll only promise not to punish him!"

"Never mind, Quin, let him beat me if he likes; it doesn't much matter. I'm sure *you* needn't beg for me, for I've only done you harm."

"Wait a while, Mr. Hardy," interrupted Mr. Lynton. "Why did you not ask your father for the money, Tom?"

"Because I knew he wouldn't give it to me. I expected there'd be no end of a row when it was discovered, but I didn't mean the blame to fall on him," and he pointed over his shoulder to Philip; "I thought he would have spent the money before now, too."

"And you actually braved your father's anger, and committed this theft, to do Philip Quin a kindness?" For the first time the boy faltered, and was silent.

"This is a very strange story, Mr. Hardy, and yet I am bound to believe it. I am also much pained to find that you have deceived me with regard to Quin. You are aware that

before I left home some weeks ago, I had a
conversation with you on the subject; and
you then professed yourself so well satisfied
with the lad, that you agreed to increase his
salary from that date; this I find you have
not done. After what has occurred to-day
(if Mrs. Quin will permit me to take this
matter into my own hands), Philip will no
longer remain in your service; and if your
word is of any value, the note is still his by
rights—the arrears of his hard-won earnings
for the past five weeks—and you are yet six
dollars in his debt for the present one."
Hardy, biting his lips to control his passion,
threw down the money on the table and stalked
out of the room without more ado; his son
was about to follow, when Mr. Lynton held
out his hand to him. "As for you, Tom,
you have done very wrong, but I believe you
did it thoughtlessly, and under a strong sense
of the injustice done to Philip. If you come
up to Lyntonville to-morrow, I shall be glad
to speak to you."

When they were left alone, Harry's joy
could brook no further restraints. He clapped
his hands, and capered about in the most
eccentric manner.

"Philip, my boy, I congratulate you," said
Mr. Lynton, shaking him warmly by the

hand, "and you also, my dear madam; and now I think a little change of scene and rest after all this trouble and annoyance will do you no harm, so if you will kindly put up anything you may require, I will come round in half an hour and drive you both back with me. Mrs. Lynton is already prepared to welcome you, for I sent off a messenger some time ago, though I hardly hoped then we should have been so cheerful."

Very shortly after the happy party were all assembled once more in the hospitable old homestead of Lyntonville.

CHAPTER XI.

" I saw that I was lost, far gone astray ;
    No hope of safe return there seemed to be ;
But then I heard that Jesus was the Way,
    A new and living way prepared for me."

THE change was so pleasant to Philip, that
he could scarcely realise at first his freedom
from hard work and the watchful eye of his
harsh master ; and when Mr. Lynton took him
into his library, and pointed out a number of
shelves from which he might choose any
book he liked, his delight knew no bounds.
Was it possible that his weary shop-boy life
was over, and he had leisure once more to
return to his much-loved studies ? But
in a day or two the reaction came, and the
exciting events of the past week in particular
began to tell on his feeble frame.

Nothing was heard of Tom Hardy next
day until Harry returned from school with
the news that he had left the village, no one
seemed to know why or wherefore. For a
time, Philip seemed to be gradually re-

covering, but when the severe cold set in, and he was no longer able to leave the house, the slight improvement was checked, and he became very ill.   Mr. and Mrs. Lynton would not hear of his leaving their hospitable roof, for they knew he needed tender nursing, and many comforts which his mother's slender means could not afford.

"No, my dear friend," Mrs. Lynton would say, "you know it is quite an acquisition to us to have such an addition to our party in this dreary winter weather, and Harry is so delighted at having a companion again that it would be quite cruel to leave him alone at present."   The widow's eyes would fill with tears, as she thanked the kind friends whom God had raised up for her in her sore distress.   For a dark shadow hung over her. Her son, her only son was passing away, as she feared, before her eyes, and it seemed as though the light of her life would be quenched. It became necessary soon to keep Philip a close prisoner to his room, for the only chance of saving him seemed to be to nurse him carefully through the long winter, and his fond mother clung to the hope that new health and life might come to her boy with the breath of the sweet spring-time.   Harry spent the greater part of his leisure with his

friend, and helped to cheer him with his
unfailing mirth and high spirits. He never
thought for a moment that Philip was in
any danger, so his merry laugh rang out
clear as ever, as he rushed into his room
with some tale of school-life, full of boisterous glee and rude health.

One day he was running home as fast as
usual, when he saw a boy skulking about
near the house, and to his surprise Tom
Hardy came up.

" I've been watching for you this long
time, Lynton ; tell me how Quin is ! "

" Why, where have you sprung from,
Hardy ? I thought you had gone away ! "
said Harry, without answering his question,
and wondering at his gaunt looks, so
different from the last time they met.

" Well, you see, I'm here now, at any rate;
but I want to know—how's Quin ? "

" He's very ill," said Harry, looking
grave.

" Where is he now ? Up here ? " said
Hardy, with a nod of his head in the
direction of the house.

" Yes, they've been here ever since."

" But tell me, Lynton, he isn't going to
—to die ? " said Tom, with quivering lips.

Harry looked at him with astonishment,

the idea had never struck him, but he did not like it nevertheless. "No," he answered shortly, "of course not!"

"I wonder if I —"

"Why, Hardy, what's the matter?" asked Lynton, in surprise, for the boy was so unlike his former self that even "careless Harry" could not fail to be struck by it.

"I don't know—I'm very hungry."

"Why, man, come along; why didn't you say so before? I'll find something for you!" cried Harry, "here, this way!" and he led him towards the house. At the door Mr. Lynton met them.

"Tom Hardy! you here; is it possible?" said he.

"I'm going to get him something to eat, papa, he says he's hungry."

"I've had no food to-day, and scarce any yesterday,' said Hardy, "or I wouldn't ask."

"Poor fellow! why, how is this, Hardy? But come in, you are not in a fit state to answer questions," and Mr. Lynton brought him in, while Harry busied himself in getting a comfortable meal provided for his former schoolfellow.

"And now, Hardy, come into the library, and tell me all about it," said Mr. Lynton, rising when he had finished. Tom followed

him into the snug, warm room. " I expected to see you again after the last time
we met, but Harry came home and told us
that you had disappeared. What happened
then ? "

" Didn't you hear, sir, that my father
turned me out of doors ? He told me that
if I ever dared to come into his sight again,
he would have me taken up and put in
prison ; so I ran away that night. Jack
managed to put up some of my clothes for
me on the sly, and I had a little money. I
walked as far as the ' Four Corners,' where
the stage stopped, and got a lift on to Midborough."

" And what did you do when you got
there ? "

" Well, sir, I scarcely know how I have
lived this last two months, but I got errands,
and one thing and another, so that I didn't
starve : and a woman who once lived about
here, gave me lodging for a trifle, and a
dinner too, sometimes—but it was hard
work."

" But what brought you back here, Tom ?"

The boy looked down, and hesitated. His
lips were no strangers to a lie ; but Philip's
life had not been without its effect upon him.
He had been kept from stealing many a time,

when sore pressed by hunger, by the memory of his patient endurance ; and now he has been drawn back to the neighbourhood chiefly by a rumour of Philip's serious illness, which had reached him by chance at Midborough. He felt he must confess, for the weight on his conscience was more than he could bear. Philip might be dying, and he must ask his forgiveness before it was too late. Mr. Lynton's kind words too, had not been thrown away, and he did not fear to meet him again, but he was not prepared to unburden his mind to him. He could not tell Mr. Lynton why he was there, without betraying his secret. Mr. Lynton, surprised at his confusion, repeated his question.

" I—I want to see Quin," he blurted out at length.

" Well, you shall see him presently," said Mr. Lynton, kindly; " but what are you going to do with yourself afterwards ? "

" I don't know ; going back, I suppose," said Tom, rather dubiously.

" Well, I must see what can be done; perhaps I may be able to find some employment for you—come in," he added, as Harry knocked at the door.

" Philip wants to see Hardy, papa, when you have done with him."

"You can go now, Tom," said Mr. Lynton ; and Harry led the way to the room which Philip occupied. The sofa on which he was lying was drawn towards the window, and the pale crescent of the new moon shone in, in the cold grey twilight of a winter's afternoon. Philip held out his wasted hand as Hardy entered, and Harry left them together. "I'm sorry you're so bad, Quin," said Hardy, looking frightened and pale, and beginning to repent of his resolution to confess—it seemed so much more difficult now that the time had come.

"I wanted so much to see you, Hardy ; you don't mind coming up, do you ? I've been ill, and sometimes I think I shall never be any better ; and I thought I should like to give you this," said Philip, laying his hand on the Bible by his side, which Mr. Elmslie had given him, and Tom had saved from the fire. "See, I have written your name in it, and Hardy, you will keep it and read it for my sake, won't you ?" he added, earnestly. "Dear Tom, will you promise me ?"

"Oh, I can't!—I can't have it!" sobbed the boy, quite broken down by Philip's pleading words. "I've done you more harm than any one else ever did, and I can't! I can't!"

" Oh, Hardy, you will? It is the last thing, most likely, I shall ever ask you, and you won't refuse me? I know you will not."

Tom rose from his low seat by Philip's side, and, calming himself, spoke rapidly and with a strong effort.

" Stay, you don't know all, wait till you hear, and then you will hate and despise me as I hate and despise myself now; but I must tell—I came here to tell you, for I can't keep it to myself any longer, and I don't care what becomes of me! I burnt down your place there, I did! because I hated to see you getting the prizes and keeping above me in the class. Do you hear?" said he, seeing Philip looked neither surprised nor indignant, " I tell you 'twas I set fire to your arbour that night! I didn't mean to burn the cottage, but it caught. It was I ruined you, Quin, and brought all this trouble upon you, and if you die I shall feel I have killed you: and now you know all!" His forced composure gave way, and hiding his face in his hands, he sobbed as if his heart would break. There was silence in the room for a minute, broken only by the sound of Hardy's weeping; and then Philip laid his hand gently on his arm.

" Dear Hardy, I have known all this a long

THE CONFESSION.

123

time ! " The boy looked up in blank amaze-
ment. " Yes," continued Philip, " I suspected it from the very first, and I'll tell you
why. Do you remember losing your knife
about that time ? "

" Yes," said Hardy, " and I searched and
searched for it again and again."

" Well, I picked it up where you had
dropped it that night, and I have ever since
been pretty nearly sure that you did it. I let
the knife fall into the hollow tree up by Long
Acre afterwards."

" And you never told ? "

" No," said Philip ; " I was very angry at
first, but then I thought how it was—that it
was worse than you meant it to be—so I have
always kept the secret. I did not mean to
tell you now, only you spoke yourself."

" Oh ! Quin, how could you ? And you
worked so hard, and were accused of stealing,
too, when you knew it was all my doing ;
and you never spoke a word ! "

" I prayed that God would help me,
Hardy, and He did. I was very near telling
two or three times, though. If I had not
had strength given me I should have done
so."

" But, Quin, why didn't you speak up ?
My father would have been obliged to make

it all straight ; and besides, you'd have had your revenge ! "

" I have had my revenge," said Philip, smiling ; but Hardy broke down again :—

" Oh ! Quin, if I had only known ! I believe you are really good—I do. But I've been taught to sneer and scoff, until I scarcely know right from wrong. To think that you should have known it all the time, and never spoke ! Oh ! I wish I could be good like you—I'm so miserable—but I never shall be, I'm too wicked for that ; and I've got a fit punishment for burning you out, for now I've no home to go to. I wish I were dead, that I do ! "

" Oh ! Tom, don't say that," said Philip, " it makes me shudder to hear you speak so wickedly. Think what a solemn thing it is to die ! Are you ready to appear in the presence of God, and to give an account of all you have done in this world ? Dear Tom, you have confessed your fault to me, but let me ask you—have you ever thought of confessing your sins to God, and a.. .ing Him to pardon you for Christ's sake ? "

" No," said Tom, " I never thought of that, Philip ; you know I was not brought up as you have been. We were never taught much about God, except in our lessons at school, and I tried to think as little of them as I could, after they were said. I did not think God would care for what I did."

"God cares for all, dear Tom ; He not only made the world, He rules it, too. ' His eyes are in every place, beholding the evil and the good.' He sees all that we *think*, as well as all that we *do;* He hears every word we say, and He has said that not only for every evil deed, but for ' every idle word that men shall speak, they shall give account in the day of judgment.' "

Tom looked anxiously at Philip. "Then what is to become of me ? " said he ; " I have been so wicked and have done so much evil. You are happy, Philip, you have always been good, you are sure to go to heaven—but what is to become of me ? "

"I am not good, Tom ; and if I could only get to heaven by my own goodness, I would never get there at all. I feel that I am a sinner, that there is no good thing in me, and my only hope of being saved is through what our Lord Jesus Christ has done for us. He died on the cross to save us poor sinners. I trust in Him alone, and He will save you, too, if you ask Him."

"I learned that at school," said Tom, " but I never thought much about it. I did not think then that I was a sinner. I had not done anything very bad till I burnt your house; and you know, Philip, that I did not mean to do such a wicked thing, I only meant to burn the summer-house, and you could easily have built that again. But somehow, ever since then, I seem to have been going from bad to worse. I am bad enough now, I feel that. But still I think you have been good, Philip; you have been an honest boy and a good son."

"Even if my outward conduct had been quite good," said Philip, "which it has not always been, still my heart has been wicked. Sin ruled in my heart by nature, as it does in the heart of every unrenewed sinner; and though I trust that I am pardoned for Christ's sake, and I strive against sin as a thing He hates, yet I feel daily need of forgiveness, and pray daily that God would grant me His Holy Spirit, to purify my heart and keep me from evil."

"What do you mean by 'every unrenewed sinner?'" asked Tom.

"Everyone who has not become a new creature by having his sinful nature changed by the Holy Spirit, and his sins washed away by the blood of Christ. All need this change, and none can be saved without it, for our

Lord himself has said, 'Except a man be born again, he cannot see the kingdom of God.'"

"But will God change my heart?" said Tom; "am I not too bad to become really good now?"

"Our Lord Jesus Christ welcomes all, even the worst, even the chief of sinners. He says: 'I am not come to call the righteous, but sinners to repentance,' and 'him that cometh unto me I will in no wise cast out.' You will find many such promises in God's word. That's why I want you to have my Bible; it's God's message to us, you know, and it teaches us what we must do. You will read it, won't you?—and then you will love it as I do."

"Well, I will for your sake, otherwise I should hate to look at it, because it was partly envy about it that made me do wrong at first. But did the Bible teach you not to tell?—I don't understand."

Philip opened his little Testament and pointed out several passages. They sat and talked together some time, and at last Hardy said:

"I suppose I must go now, and I needn't show my face to Mr. Lynton again, for you'll tell now, Philip?"

"Oh! Hardy, do tell yourself, you will feel so much happier, I am sure you will."

"Well, but Mr. Lynton said he would try to help me, and he won't do it if I tell; but if you don't mind keeping the secret, Philip, as you have done for so long," and a gleam of hope brightened his face, "perhaps he will; and I'm half-starved now."

Philip looked troubled. "It wouldn't be right, Hardy, indeed it would not. You must tell him, and I know he won't be angry, for he is so kind; oh! do, please do, tell him yourself!"

"But, Quin, I can't, he'd be so awfully angry. I'd much rather go away and shift for myself."

"He won't be angry, Hardy; and if you like I'll tell him for you, if you stay here; oh! do let me."

"But your mother, Philip, and all of them, they will never forgive me; no, let me go away, I can get on somehow. They think I'm bad enough as it is, without this."

"No, they will not; I won't let you go away, Hardy. Mother!" he cried, as he heard her light step in the adjoining room, "come and sit down here by me a little while, here's Tom Hardy, I know you'll be glad to see him:" and very gently, and little by

little, he helped Hardy to make his confession.
Mrs. Quin was much astonished as the truth
dawned upon her; but his evident distress
and sorrow disarmed every feeling of resent-
ment, and only thankfulness for the noble
conduct of her boy remained. Mr. Lynton
was told the whole story, and though he spoke
very seriously to Hardy, it was not in displeasure, nor did he retract his promise of
endeavouring to find him some suitable employment. Hardy could never forget Philip's
kindness, or the earnest, pleading words he
had spoken. The memory of that interview
remained with him till his dying hour, and
from that time he became an altered character. We do not mean that he suddenly
became good, and pious, and unselfish; but
that day was the turning-point in his life,
and Philip was the instrument, in God's
hands, of working this happy change in one
hitherto so unpromising.

Suitable occupation was eventually obtained
for Tom, but not before he had been reconciled to his father, through the kind inter-
cession of Mr. Lynton; but Mr. Hardy
having expressed a wish that he should have
an opportunity of gaining experience else-
where before settling again in Fairfield, Tom
returned to Midborough, where he remained

some years. Happily he fell into good hands,
and as time advanced he was enabled, by the
grace of God, to overcome the disadvantages
of his early associations. If we take a glance
into the future, we shall see that he has so
far gained the esteem and approbation of his
fellow-citizens in a commendable and successful career, that if circumstances do not
belie the expectations of his most sanguine
friends, he will yet b..ar in the Legislative
Council of his country the well-merited title
of the Honourable T. Hardy !

CHAPTER XII.

CONCLUSION.

"Be still, sad heart, and cease repining,
Behind the cloud is the sun still shining."

"Weeping may endure for a night, but joy cometh
in the morning."

MARCH had set in with hard frosts and keen biting winds, but every one rejoiced that the long winter was nearly over; and as Philip seemed no worse than he had been for some months, hope began to grow strong in his mother's heart. But the doctor shook his head.

"I fear the month of May more than anything for him," he said one day to Mrs. Lynton; "the sudden changes of our climate are so trying to patients of this class. A sea-voyage might save him, but I've not said so before, for in Mrs. Quin's circumstances, it must be out of the question."

Philip, who was inclined to be rather desponding by nature, had long given up all

hopes of recovering; and his most sorrowful
thought was of the parting with his mother,
and leaving her to fight the hard battle of
life alone. Often they would read together
the descriptions of the heavenly land to which
he seemed to be hastening, where there would
be no more sorrow, or parting, and where
tears would be wiped from every eye. But
the parting was not so near as Philip and his
widowed mother feared, for the chastening
hand which it had pleased God to lay upon
them for so long, was about to be removed,
and brighter days were in store.

Not many days after Dr. Ford's last visit,
a large packet of letters which had arrived by
the last English mail was brought in and
laid before Mr. Lynton, as the custom of the
house was, when the party were all assembled
at breakfast. Every one was soon occupied
in reading their own, when a sudden excla-
mation of surprise from Mr. Lynton attracted
the attention of all.

" Well, this is passing strange—indeed, I
may say providential! My dear Madam, let
me congratulate you most warmly," said he,
rising and shaking hands heartily with Mrs.
Quin, who thought for a moment he must
have taken leave of his senses. "I have
good news for you. I am informed that your

son, Philip Walter Quin, has just fallen heir to the property, real and personal, of his uncle, Captain W. P. Quin, who died suddenly on the tenth of April last. A long and fruitless search has been made for him, and now this letter is sent to me as the magistrate of this district, making inquiries concerning the whereabouts of the said Philip Quin, who is supposed to be living somewhere in the neighbourhood, as his presence is required at once, if possible, in England. I think," he added, smiling, " I shall be able to give the requisite information ! "

Astonishment took the place of every other feeling in Mrs. Quin's mind at these unexpected tidings.

" But are you sure this is true?" she said, "for one chief cause of our leaving Ireland, and our consequent troubles, was an unhappy quarrel between my husband and his brother, and any hopes of help from that quarter, I had entirely given up for years. "

" Nevertheless it is undoubtedly true," replied Mr. Lynton, " for here are full particulars from his solicitor ! "

Mrs. Quin took the letter ; but her eyes were blinded by the fast-falling tears, as she thought that if this good news had only come in time, her son might have been spared to her.

"Oh!" cried Mrs. Lynton, when she understood it all, "how thankful I am! It was only the other day Dr. Ford told me that a sea-voyage might yet save Philip, and I believe it will." The widow caught eagerly at her cheering words, and when the doctor came in later in the day and confirmed her most sanguine hopes, her joy and gratitude to the gracious Giver of all good things know no bounds.

"But you must break it to him very cautiously," said he, "for any great excitement in his weak state might prove fatal; and the greatest care will be necessary in the land journey. Once get him to the sea, and there is not so much to fear."

It was some time before the widowed mother could realize her happiness, for she hardly dared to believe that her beloved son might yet be spared to her. As she grew accustomed to the idea and felt that their bitter days of poverty were over, her joy seemed almost too great.

"How can I ever thank you, my dear, kind friends, for all you have done for me and mine?" she said. "Without your generous sympathy, our life would indeed have been sad—strangers and poor in a foreign land; but God will reward you!"

No one rejoiced more unfeignedly in the welcome tidings than Harry, and he showed his glee in the most characteristic manner. It was all they could do to prevent his rushing up to Philip at once and telling him the whole story in his excited way, but as this was most strictly and seriously forbidden, he was obliged to content himself with fidgeting in and out of his room, and continually bursting out into little fits of ecstacy, rubbing his hands, and muttering to himself, "Oh, isn't it jolly!" Then, suddenly remembering that a weighty secret was entrusted to his keeping which he was on no account to divulge, he would try to look grave and pull a long face, until the next happy thoughts of his friend's good fortune would set him off again. It must be confessed that all this was rather trying to the young invalid, who being un-acquainted with the cause of his odd behaviour wondered what could possess his light-hearted companion. But Harry's patience was not destined to be put to a very severe test. Towards evening, Mrs. Quin went up to sit with Philip in the twilight as was her wont; and for a few moments after her first loving inquiries, they were silent, his thin hand resting in the warm, loving embrace of hers.

"God has been very merciful to us, my darling," she said softly, at length, as he leant his head against her.

"Yes," he answered; but he spoke sadly, for he was thinking of the parting which seemed so near: then he looked up in her face, as the flame from the open stove glanced upon it in the dim light, and he saw that though her eyes were glistening with tears, it wore a joyful expression. "What is it, mother? something has happened!"

"I have just received the news of your uncle Walter's death, Philip."

"Oh, mother! but that does not make you glad, does it?"

"God forgive me!" thought she, "I have been selfish in my joy." "No, my boy," she said aloud, "though I never saw him; but, Philip, it alters our circumstances very much."

"Oh, I am so glad, so thankful! Now I shall die without a care, if I think you are provided for. God has indeed been good to us!" And the tears rolled down his face.

"Yes, darling; and suppose you were to get well, Philip; suppose it were now in our power to use the only means of doing you good?"

"Mother," said he, "you would not say

so if you had not good hopes—tell me, oh,
do tell me, is it true ?"

"My son, in God's great mercy, I believe
it is," she replied, solemnly. "I would not,
you know I would not, be so cruel as to raise
false hopes ; but Dr. Ford assures me that a
sea-voyage may yet restore you, and now,
thank God, we can go."

"Oh, I am thankful, mother, dear mother!
It would have been hard to part; but if I am
spared, may God give me grace to live more
to His glory, and to be a greater comfort to
you than I have been !" The room grew
darker and darker, but there was light and
joy in their hearts, such as they had not
known for many long days ; and the mother
and son rejoiced together in their great
happiness.

Little more remains to be told. Mr.
Lynton had been long wishing for an opportunity of sending Harry to finish his education in England, and though his parents
were grieved at the thought of parting with
him, yet they would not lose so good an
opportunity ; so it was arranged that he
should accompany Mrs. Quin and Philip.
Great care was taken of the young invalid,
and they reached Quebec by short and easy
stages. The journey did not try him so

much even as they expected, and with the
first breath of sea-air came a change for the
better.   They arrived in Liverpool after a
prosperous voyage, and soon after proceeded
to London, where Harry sorrowfully bade
them farewell before entering alone upon the
new and varied experiences of an English
public school.   He often missed Philip's
ready advice and help, and right glad was he
when they met again once more.   It was in
Mrs. Quin's pleasant country residence that
his happy holidays were spent.   Here was
his second home, and he loved to call it so.

Philip by this time had regained even
more than his former health, and when
Harry's holidays were over, he returned with
him, to contest once more for the double
honours of class and playground.   The discipline of their early days was not lost upon
either of them, and Philip especially never
regretted the lessons of self-dependence and
self-sacrifice which he had been taught in
the stern school of adversity.

And is there no truth that our young
readers may learn from the little story we
have related ?   We think there is.   The
word of God tells us that "None of us liveth
to himself."   Each word and action of even
the very youngest must exercise some in-

fluence for evil or for good on those around
them; and we have seen how Philip's quiet,
consistent conduct was the means, in God's
hands, of leading one who seemed in every
way most unpromising, to seek for pardon
and peace through our Saviour Christ, who
alone can bestow it.

The work which God gives each one of us,
young and old, to do, lies close to our hand;
and though the path of duty is sometimes
rugged and steep, calling for patient self-
denial, yet if we strive by God's grace to go
straight forward in it, He will surely make
use of our silent example for His own glory
and the good of those about us.

Years after, when Philip revisited the
scenes of his boyish trials, and once more
renewed his acquaintance with his old companion and former foe, Tom Hardy—now
become a good and worthy man—he was able
to look back upon his early discipline with
thankfulness, and to feel that it had not been
in vain that so many of his early days had
been spent in the forest shades of

LYNTONVILLE.

UNWIN BROTHERS, PRINTERS, BUCKLERSBURY, E.C.